*The world is indeed full of peril, and in it there are
many dark places; but still there is much that is fair,
and though in all lands love is now mingled with grief,
it grows perhaps the greater.*

J. R. R. Tolkien, The Fellowship of the Ring

FATES OF VEILORE NOVELLA

RUIN OF HIS HEART

IRELAND LYDON

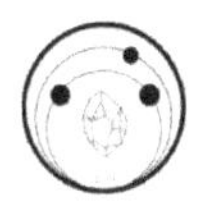

AN IMPRINT OF VEILORE PRESS

ISBN: 9798990265196 (Paperback)

First Printing Edition 2026

To the healers who walk among us,
Bearers of knowledge, guardians of fragile breath.

With steady hands and steadfast hearts,
You mend what fate would fray.
In the quiet battles fought in sterile halls,
You are the keepers of hope.

For your skill, your courage, and your mercy,
We offer our deepest thanks.

RUIN OF HIS HEART

DEAR READER,

November 20, 1999

What follows is not a history in the strictest sense, but a record of recollection.

The account contained within these pages has been drawn from numerous interviews conducted with Mr. Isaac Peter Maison during the course of his confinement and treatment. The narrative is, in essence, his own telling. Memory, as any physician of the mind understands, is an imperfect instrument. Dates may blur. Certain moments appear with unnatural clarity, while others vanish entirely into manic episodes. For this reason, the chronology and specific identifications contained in this document should be regarded as impressions rather than certainties.

Yet the substance of the events themselves cannot be dismissed so easily.

In the months since these interviews began, I have spoken with several individuals connected to Mr. Maison's life. Conversations with Mr. Malcolm Howard Dawson, Mr. Neil Maison, and Mr. Thomas Hidestone have illuminated portions of the account that might otherwise have remained obscured. In several instances their testimonies have aligned with the patient's recollection in ways that are difficult to attribute solely to coincidence or delusion.

It is my professional duty to acknowledge that these parallels raise questions that medicine alone cannot comfortably answer.

Repeated attempts have been made to contact Mr. Anthony Mooren concerning both the illness of his sister and his past association with Mr. Maison. At the time of this writing, he has declined all correspondence and has offered no statement regarding the matters described herein. His silence, intentional or otherwise, leaves a portion of the narrative suspended without confirmation.

I present this document not as a definitive account of events, but as a record of testimony gathered from a mind that insists upon its own truth. Whether the reader chooses to regard these pages as the product of fractured memory, coincidence, or something less easily explained must remain a matter of personal judgment.

Nevertheless, after reviewing the statements of those involved, I cannot wholly dismiss the possibility that beneath the distortions of memory there exists a reality far stranger than the one we are prepared to accept.

Dr. Nicholas Fielder
Attending Physician

BEFORE

SEPTEMBER 16, 1999 – 10:42 A.M.

PATIENT NAME: ISAAC PETER MAISON

> **DATE OF BIRTH:** JUNE 23, 1976

> **PLACE OF BIRTH:** GREENWICH, LONDON

FAMILY:

> SON OF CHARLES GREY MAISON AND ELEANOR MAISON (DE-CEASED, 1983).

> IDENTICAL TWIN BROTHER: HENRY JAMES MAISON.

CURRENT GUARDIAN:

> NEIL MAISON (UNCLE), APPOINTED DUE TO PATIENT'S LACK OF CAPACITY DURING ONGOING TREATMENT.

> SEE APPENDIX I.A REGARDING DOCUMENTED PSYCHOSIS.

RESIDENCE: HARROW

PHYSICAL DESCRIPTION:

> MALE. HAIR BLACK, OILY, AND UNKEMPT AT THE TIME OF ASSESSMENT. EYES GREEN. COMPLEXION PALE OLIVE.

I really don't see how this is going to help," Isaac interrupted, his voice low and sharp, cutting across the steady cadence of the man behind the mahogany desk.

Dr. Fielder paused, glancing over the rim of his glasses at the sullen figure slouched in the high-backed chair opposite him. Isaac's dark flannel shirt hung loose over his wiry frame, and his faded, torn denim jeans were almost threadbare. Despite the layers, the young man's gaunt features betrayed his frailty.

"It is customary," Dr. Fielder began, maintaining the practiced calm of his voice, "to read aloud my client's details to ensure there are no errors or discrepancies."

Isaac scoffed, looking away. "Do we really have to talk about what I look like? I mean, you can see me."

Dr. Fielder folded his hands, steepling his fingers as he leaned back. His gaze remained steady, assessing. "You understand this is for the recording," he replied, gesturing briefly toward the tape recorder on the side table, its reel turning with a soft, mechanical hum.

Isaac's eyes flicked toward it, then away, his lips tightening in silence.

"Tell me about Penelope," Dr. Fielder pressed.

Isaac's reaction was immediate. His green eyes snapped toward the doctor, the intensity of his glare sharp enough to make Dr. Fielder feel it in his chest. Isaac's jaw clenched, teeth grinding audibly.

"We can revisit that another time," Dr. Fielder offered, his voice steady. He glanced back at his notes. "Where was I... ah, yes."

FORMER RESIDENCE:

CAMDEN PLACE, SHARED WITH ADOPTIVE BROTHER MALCOLM HOWARD DAWSON.

ADOPTIVE BROTHER:

MALCOLM HOWARD DAWSON, BORN AUGUST 4, 1976, TO CHELSEA STONE AND FATHER UNKNOWN.

Raised by maternal grandmother Rosaline Stone until her death in 1964.

Mr. Dawson remains a secondary caretaker in the event of medical emergencies.

Evaluation:

This assessment has been conducted to determine the terms of the patient's possible release. The patient may be placed in institutional care or returned to guardianship pending the results of the final interview. Until such determination is made, the patient will remain in hospital custody.

"There now," Dr. Fielder said, setting his notes aside and removing his glasses. He leaned forward slightly, the clock on the wall filling the silence with its relentless ticking. "Have you any remarks on what I've just read?"

Isaac sat unmoving, the only response a faint shift in his posture.

"This interview," Dr. Fielder continued, "and all you share with me will determine your path forward. Do you wish to return to the facility, Isaac? I understand you spent many years there after the tragedy of losing your mother and brother."

Isaac's cold glare intensified, his green eyes locked onto the doctor with a chilling rigidity that made Dr. Fielder sit a little straighter.

"I cannot imagine what you've endured," Dr. Fielder said softly, his tone measured. "But your uncle has arranged this because he cares for you. He doesn't want to see you harmed. Even if it means intervening before you harm yourself."

"Talking won't bring them back," Isaac muttered, his voice low and hollow.

Dr. Fielder sighed, adjusting the papers in his lap. "No," he admitted. "But talking about them might bring you back. That's why we're here, Isaac. To bring you back."

As the silence stretched, Isaac's hands curled into fists on the worn arms of the chair, his knuckles pale against the fabric. Dr. Fielder waited, his steady gaze unwavering, until the tension in the room became almost unbearable.

"I'm not broken," Isaac said finally, his voice sharp but brittle, like a shard of glass about to snap.

"No one said you were," Dr. Fielder replied calmly, leaning forward slightly. "But you are hurting, and you're here because someone cares enough to help you. Whether you accept that help is up to you."

Isaac let out a hollow laugh, his head tilting back as he stared at the ornate ceiling. "Help," he said bitterly. "Like locking me away helped when I was eight? Like drugging me helped? Like pretending I didn't exist helped?" His voice rose with each word, his eyes blazing as they snapped back to the doctor. "They all helped so much, didn't they?"

Dr. Fielder didn't flinch. He had seen this anger before, this volcanic eruption born of grief and fear. "It sounds like you've been carrying this weight for a very long time," he said softly.

"Don't," he warned, Isaac's laugh came again, more strained this time. "Don't talk to me like I'm some case study. You don't know me."

"You're right," Dr. Fielder said, surprising Isaac into silence. "I don't know you—not yet. But I'd like to. Because you deserve to be known, Isaac. You deserve more than the pain you're drowning in."

The young man's jaw worked, his teeth grinding audibly again. His eyes darted to the side table, to the recording device, then back to the doctor.

"Why Penelope?" Isaac asked suddenly, his voice tight.

Dr. Fielder folded his hands in his lap, keeping his expression neutral. "You've mentioned her name in previous sessions, always in moments of heightened distress. It seems she's important to you."

Isaac's mouth twisted, his hands flexing against the chair's arms. For a moment, it seemed he might explode again, but instead, his voice came out quiet, almost a whisper. "She doesn't belong here. Not in this."

Dr. Fielder nodded. "Then tell me where she belongs. Help me understand why she matters to you."

Isaac's breathing hitched, his gaze dropping to his hands, which had unclenched and now rested limply on the arms of the chair. "She was the only thing that made it better," he said, his voice barely above a whisper. His eyes fixed on the space between them, unfocused, as though he were looking at something only he could see. "After Henry, after our mum... Penelope was the only light I had left."

Dr. Fielder leaned forward slightly, careful not to break the fragile thread of trust beginning to form. "What happened to her?" he asked gently.

Isaac's throat worked as he swallowed, his lips pressing into a thin line. His voice, when it came, was cracked and raw. "Cancer." The word fell like a stone into the stillness of the room.

Dr. Fielder didn't respond immediately, allowing the weight of Isaac's confession to settle. When he spoke, his tone was measured and soft. "That must have been devastating for you."

Isaac let out a bitter laugh, sharp and jagged. "Devastating doesn't cover it," he said, his green eyes shimmering with unshed tears. "She fought so hard, you know? Through all the treatments, all the pain. She never let me see how bad it was, not until the end."

He paused, his hands clenched into fists again. "She made me promise to keep going. To live. As if that was some kind of gift she was giving me by dying." His voice broke on the last word, and he looked away, biting down on his lip hard enough to draw blood.

"She sounds like she was an incredible person," the doctor said.

"She was," Isaac murmured, his voice barely audible. "She deserved better. She deserved to live."

"And you blame yourself," Dr. Fielder said, his voice gentle but probing.

Isaac froze, his knuckles turning white around the arm of the chair. "Doesn't everyone?" he muttered. "Isn't that what people do when someone dies? Blame the ones left behind?"

Dr. Fielder shook his head. "No, Isaac. Most people grieve, but they don't blame themselves for things they couldn't control. Penelope's illness wasn't your fault. You didn't give her cancer, and you couldn't have cured it. Her death was a tragedy, but it wasn't on you."

Isaac's laugh came again, hollow and bitter. "Yeah, well, try telling that to the part of me that won't shut up about how useless I was. She was everything, and I couldn't save her. Just like I couldn't save Henry. Or mum."

Dr. Fielder let a moment of silence stretch between them, his gaze steady. "You've lost so much, Isaac," he said softly. "But holding onto that guilt—it's like carrying a weight you were never meant to bear. Penelope wanted you to live. Not just survive, but live. Maybe it's time to start thinking about what that means."

Isaac didn't respond. He stared at the water glass that sat untouched before him, his green eyes distant. After a long pause, his voice heavy with exhaustion. "I don't even know what that looks like anymore."

PART ONE

1

London, England. 1995.

I saac hunched over the cold porcelain toilet in the dimly lit bathroom, his body heaving from the remnants of another nightmare. The same dripping visions that turned his blood cold had clawed him from his restless sleep yet again. Blinking against the grogginess, he wiped his mouth with the back of his hand and leaned back on his heels. His unkempt hair fell into his eyes, and he shoved it away with a trembling hand, shivering as the chill of the room seeped into his bones.

Another sleepless night. Another unwelcome reminder that the nightmares never truly left him.

Standing unsteadily, Isaac gripped the edge of the sink for balance, his breaths shallow and uneven. He closed his eyes, focusing on each inhale, each exhale, counting them in a futile attempt to regain control. But his hand betrayed him, shaking violently.

Without thinking, he swung open the mirrored medicine cabinet. His fingers quickly found the small, hidden compartment at the back. Inside was a battered bottle of pills. Pain meds from an old prescription. His lifeline when the memories became too raw, the shakes too relentless.

With a click, he closed the cabinet, staring at his reflection again. His pale, hollow face seemed to mock him.

"You're fine," he muttered under his breath, though he didn't believe it.

The sound of the faucet broke the heavy silence as he turned it on, splashing cold water over his face. Today was supposed to be different. Anthony had insisted on taking them to the ballet, claiming it was important to support his sister's performance. Isaac didn't want to go. He didn't want to see anyone, let alone be crammed into a theater with strangers. But Anthony had been adamant, and Isaac didn't have the energy to fight him on it.

Hours later, Isaac sat on the bus, pressed beside Anthony and Malcom. His knee bounced restlessly, his leg shaking with a rhythm he couldn't stop. He counted each stop in his head, trying to drown out the chatter of the other passengers. The world felt too loud, too bright, pressing in on him from all sides. He clenched his jaw, waiting for the pills to kick in.

When the familiar numbness finally washed over him, he exhaled, his muscles loosening slightly. The constant thrum of anxiety dulled, leaving only a vague sense of detachment in its place. He let his head rest against the window, the cool glass soothing against his temple as the bus trundled toward the theater.

The grand hall of the ballet was a blur of soft golden light and murmured conversation. Isaac followed Anthony and Malcom in silence, his head lowered to avoid meeting anyone's gaze. They were led to a box seat, high above the stage, where the view was unobstructed. As the orchestra began its overture, Isaac tried to focus on the music, letting the swelling notes carry him away from his thoughts.

But when the dancers took the stage, his attention sharpened. His eyes scanned the performers, searching, waiting. And then he saw her.

Penelope.

She moved like water, her long limbs flowing with impossible grace as she leapt onto the stage. The spotlight caught her, illuminating the soft contours of her face, her chestnut hair swept back into a tight bun. Her every step was perfection, her movements a delicate balance of strength and poise. Even after all these years, she took his breath away. He couldn't tear his eyes away, his heart thudding in his chest despite the numbing haze of the pills.

"She's stunning, isn't she?" Anthony leaned in, pointing her out as though Isaac could possibly miss her.

Isaac didn't reply. He didn't need to. His focus was locked on Penelope, every turn, every leap, every twirl. His practiced eye noted each imperfection—not hers, but her partner's. The male dancer stumbled, barely perceptible to most, but glaringly obvious to Isaac.

"Her partner's trash," Isaac muttered, his voice low but edged with annoyance.

Malcom chuckled from his other side, leaning closer. "Still holding a grudge, are we? You know he only beat you out in fourth year because his father was on the board."

Isaac's jaw tightened. He hadn't even realized the man beside Penelope was Norman, the same smug, overconfident dancer who had claimed Isaac's role all those years ago. Now jealousy gnawed at his chest, sharp and insistent.

It should have been him up there. He should have been the one lifting Penelope, matching her strength and grace with his own. Not Norman, the self-proclaimed prodigy who thought himself untouchable. Isaac's eyes followed Penelope's every move, the performance unfolding in a blur of color and music.

2

Isaac groaned as he pushed open the door to the dance studio, the familiar scent of rosin, sweat, and faintly floral air freshener hitting him like a wave of nostalgia he wasn't ready to face. The bright lights gleamed off the polished floors, and the faint echo of voices and footfalls bounced around the room. Anthony had roped him into this, again. Filling in as the pianist for a rehearsal wasn't exactly how Isaac wanted to spend his afternoon, but he owed Anthony, and a favor was a favor.

Sliding onto the piano bench, he cracked his knuckles dramatically, earning a few glances from the dancers warming up. His gaze swept across the room until it landed on Penelope. She was adjusting the ribbons on her pointe shoes, her back impossibly straight and poised even in a moment as mundane as tying knots.

Isaac's chest tightened. It had been years since he'd seen her in her element, surrounded by the art that seemed to pulse through her veins. He shoved the feeling aside, clearing his throat as the instructor, Madame Eloise, approached.

"Anthony swears you're as good as he says," she said with a raised brow, her tone skeptical but not unfriendly.

"I'm better," Isaac shot back with a lopsided grin, earning a soft chuckle from the older woman.

The practice began, and Isaac settled into the familiar rhythm of playing for dancers. His fingers moved effortlessly over the keys, the music flowing through him like second nature. It wasn't until Penelope and her partner, Norman, began their routine that he started to feel the familiar itch of irritation.

Norman was... fine. But just fine wasn't good enough. His movements were stiff, his timing slightly off, and it was throwing Penelope out of sync. She was trying to compensate for his errors, her balance wavering where it should have been effortless. Isaac's jaw tightened with each misstep.

Finally, Norman's clumsy handling of a lift caused Penelope to stumble slightly, and Isaac couldn't take it anymore. His hands crashed onto the keys in a dissonant chord that made everyone stop and look at him.

"Sorry," Isaac said, not sounding sorry at all. He stood abruptly. "But if we're going to do this, you must do it right."

Norman looked indignant, his face turning a shade of pink that clashed horribly with his sleek black practice attire. "Excuse me?"

Isaac pointed, his gaze unwavering. "You're rushing the count into the lift. She's not a sack of flour you're tossing into the air, she's the centerpiece. You're supposed to guide her, not yank her off her feet."

Madame Eloise raised a brow but said nothing, clearly intrigued by the interruption. Penelope, meanwhile, was watching Isaac with an amused glint in her eye, her lips twitching as if suppressing a smile.

Norman bristled. "I know what I'm doing—"

"No, you don't," Isaac interrupted, stepping toward the center of the room. "Here, I'll count it out for you."

He clapped out the rhythm, slow and deliberate. "One, two, three—guide. Not hurl. See the difference?"

When Norman didn't move, Isaac rolled his eyes and gestured for Penelope to take her position. "Humor me," he said, his tone dripping with mock exasperation.

Norman reluctantly complied, taking a step back, and Isaac demonstrated the sequence with an unexpected grace that left the room momentarily silent. His years of training surfaced in that moment, his body falling into the precise, flowing movements as though no time had passed since he last danced.

"Like that," he said, stepping back as Penelope landed lightly on her feet. He looked at Norman pointedly. "Your turn."

To everyone's surprise, Norman executed the lift more smoothly this time, though not without a muttered complaint. Madame Eloise clapped her hands once. "Bravo, Mr. Maison. It seems your talents extend beyond the piano."

Penelope smiled, her expression softening as she walked over to Isaac who was returning to sit at the piano. "I didn't know you still had it in you," she said, her voice low enough that only he could hear. "Impressive."

Isaac shrugged, trying to ignore the heat rising to his cheeks. "What can I say? Old habits die hard."

She tilted her head, studying him with those deep brown eyes that always seemed to see too much. "You're not half bad when you're not being insufferable."

He chuckled, leaning casually against the piano. "And you're not half bad when your partner isn't dragging you down."

Her laugh was light and melodic, and for a moment, it felt like the world had narrowed to just the two of them. "Well, maybe you should be my partner," she teased, her tone playful but with a hint of something deeper.

"I don't dance anymore," he replied, meeting her gaze.

Madame Eloise clapped her hands again, breaking the moment. "Back to positions! We don't have all day."

Penelope smirked at him before turning back to the center of the room, her movements fluid and effortless as she rejoined Norman. But as she resumed the routine, Isaac couldn't help but notice the way her gaze flicked toward him every so often, a spark of mischief in her eyes.

The afternoon sun had just begun to dip below the horizon when Penelope caught Isaac by the arm, tugging him gently toward the studio doors. The rehearsal had wrapped up without further incident, Norman grumbling to himself as he stalked off, but Penelope had remained behind, tying up loose ends with Madame Eloise. Isaac had lingered too, tinkering absently on the piano, waiting for... well, he wasn't quite sure what.

Now, as Penelope dragged him outside, her laughter ringing like wind chimes in the crisp air, he realized he didn't mind being at her mercy.

"Come on, Isaac. You owe me chips after all that," she declared, her eyes sparkling with amusement.

He arched an eyebrow, pretending to be put out. "Oh, I owe you? Last I checked, I saved that entire rehearsal from descending into mediocrity."

"And you did it so graciously," she teased, nudging him with her shoulder as they began walking down the street. "Besides, I need sustenance if I'm going to survive another minute listening to Norman complain about you."

Isaac smirked, his hands stuffed into his coat pockets. "Fair enough. Let's find the greasiest, most questionable chip shop in the area. My treat."

They ended up at a small, slightly dinghy corner shop with handwritten signs in the windows and the irresistible aroma of fried food wafting out the door. Penelope wrinkled her nose at first but grinned as Isaac held the door open for her with an exaggerated bow.

"After you, prima ballerina," he said, his tone dripping with mock reverence.

She rolled her eyes but couldn't hide her smile. "Careful, Isaac. I might get used to this level of respect."

They placed their order, one large portion of chips to share, and found a bench outside where they could sit and eat. The warm paper packet sat between them, steaming in the cool evening air as Penelope pulled out a chip and popped it into her mouth with a satisfied hum.

"So," Isaac said, watching her with a faint smile, "did Norman survive my critique, or do I need to watch my back now?"

Penelope laughed, her head tilting back as her eyes crinkled at the corners. "Oh, he'll survive. But he might be plotting your demise as we speak."

"Great," Isaac replied dryly. "I always wanted to make an enemy out of a guy with two left feet."

She nearly choked on her chip, laughing so hard that Isaac had to pat her on the back. "That's terrible," she managed between giggles. "But also... not entirely wrong."

They fell into an easy rhythm, teasing and joking as they worked their way through the chips. Every so often, their fingers would brush as they reached into the packet at the same time, and Penelope would shoot him a coy glance that made his pulse quicken.

"You know," she said after a while, leaning back against the bench, "I was actually impressed today."

"Were you?" Isaac asked, cocking an eyebrow. "With my piano skills or my unsolicited dance advice?"

"Both," she admitted, her tone playful but her gaze sincere. "I didn't realize you still danced. You looked... good out there."

Isaac felt his cheeks heat, but he shrugged nonchalantly. "It's been a while. But it's like riding a bike, I guess."

Penelope tilted her head, studying him. "Why did you stop?"

The question caught him off guard, and for a moment, he didn't know how to answer. He glanced down at the packet of chips, turning one over in his fingers before finally speaking. "Life got complicated. I am more involved with my uncle's theatre, and Anthony has started us in a band."

"Oh yes," she laughed. "Anthony's band...what did he call you all again? *Union Jack Tracks*?"

Isaac laughed, "*The Jacked Pistols*."

Her expression softened, and she nudged his shoulder gently. "Well, for what it's worth, I'm glad you haven't completely let it go. You were always... passionate about it."

Isaac looked at her, his chest tightening at the way her eyes seemed to see straight through him. "Thanks, Pen," he said softly, his usual bravado momentarily giving way to something more genuine.

She smiled, reaching for another chip. "Don't get used to the compliments. I still think you're insufferable."

He laughed, the tension easing. "Oh, I'd be worried if you didn't."

They stayed on the bench long after the chips were gone, talking and laughing as the street lights flickered on. For the first time in what felt like forever, Isaac felt lighter, he hadn't thought about taking more pills since being with her. And as Penelope playfully bumped her knee against his, he found himself wondering if maybe, just maybe, this favor he owed Anthony might lead to something more.

3

Isaac's eyes snapped open as the darkness around him melted into a kaleidoscope of twisted shadows. His heart was pounding, sweat beading on his forehead. Another nightmare, vivid and terrifying, had jolted him awake. The same face, the same echoing voice—his mother, reaching out to him from the abyss. Isaac wiped his mouth with the back of his hand, tasting the metallic tang of sweat and fear. He felt a familiar shake in his hands, the tremors that had become his constant companions over the past few months.

Fumbling in the dim light, he grabbed the bottle of pills from his nightstand. His fingers trembled as he unscrewed the cap, dropping three of the small, white tablets into his palm. Swallowing them dry, he grimaced as the bitterness coated his throat. It was always the same, a desperate attempt to snuff out the dark thoughts that haunted him.

When the numbness started to creep in, just enough to dull the edges of the fear, Isaac climbed out of bed and moved quickly. He had to get out. Out of his head, out of his apartment, away from the nightmare that was becoming his life. Pulling on his jeans and a ratty old hoodie, he brushed his hair back with a hand that shook more violently than he'd like to admit.

The bus into London was crowded, the stale smell of sweat and metal making Isaac's stomach churn. He clutched his backpack tightly, eyes scanning the seats for a vacant spot. It wasn't long before he found one, sinking into the seat and staring out the window at the blurry cityscape. The buses never seemed to be fast enough, never took him where he needed to go in time. Today was different, though. Today, he was going to meet his uncle at the theatre. Then after a real date, not just chips and flirting. Penelope had agreed to it, and Isaac was impatient to leave his demons behind and make something of this night.

The theatre was a swirl of activity when Isaac finally arrived. The air was thick with the scent of freshly cut wood, paint, and the distant hum of voices. He turned up his collar against the biting cold and pushed through the stage door, the familiar chaos comforting in its own way. His uncle, a grizzled man with a thick beard and a no-nonsense attitude, was waiting for him at the back of the house, looking through blueprints and scribbled notes.

"Isaac," his uncle greeted, his voice cutting through the background noise like a knife. "You're late."

"Sorry," Isaac mumbled, feeling the buzz of numbness start to settle in his bones. "Had a rough night."

His uncle didn't miss a beat, glancing up from the papers to give him a searching look. "Another nightmare?"

Isaac nodded, dropping heavily into a nearby chair. "Yeah. One of those nights."

"Take your meds?" his uncle asked, his tone less like a question and more of a knowing statement.

"Couple," Isaac replied, shrugging. "Just enough to get me moving."

His uncle shook his head, concern flickering in his eyes before he turned back to the plans. "You need to find something to ground you, Isaac."

"I believe Anthony has been planning on starting the band he is always talking about." Isaac shrugged, trying to fight the chill of the large room. "What are you working through?"

Neil sighed, trailing his hands along the blueprints to show Isaac the inner bones of the back of the house. "Updating this old building has become more of a pain than I had planned. But you won't be needed for this, I have a contractor on route as we speak."

"More structural problems?" Isaac asked.

"Old age has taken its toll on this old place, but keeping the charm of the older crumbling boxes has not been easy to track." Neil gave a fond glance around, before looking again at Isaac. "What shall you do today, instead of sticking around here and shouting at the young actors for forgetting their lines?"

Isaac laughed, "That was one time, Uncle, but I've got a date tonight."

That got his uncle's attention, a slow grin spreading across his face. "Oh? With Penelope?"

"Yeah," Isaac said, the corners of his mouth twitching upward in spite of himself. "Real date, not just chips."

"Well," his uncle replied, adjusting his glasses and peering over them at Isaac, "about time you did something normal. Just... don't lose yourself in it, alright?"

Isaac blew out a breath, pushing himself to his feet. "Never do."

As he stepped out of the theatre and onto the street, the chill of the London evening seemed to pierce right through him. The numbness was starting to fade, replaced by a buzzing sense of anticipation. He needed this, a moment to feel something real, something more than the relentless darkness that had been closing in on him.

Penelope shared an apartment with Anthony, that wasn't far, just a short walk away. Isaac turned up his collar, feeling the cold wind cut through him as he made his way through the maze of streets. Every step was deliberate, counting down the minutes until he would be sitting across from her, watching her smile, hearing her laugh. It was something to hold onto, a lifeline in the midst of all the chaos.

When he finally reached her apartment building, Isaac took a moment to gather himself. He smoothed his hair back, straightened his hoodie, and took a deep breath. This was going to be different. Tonight, he was going to make a memory that wasn't filled with fear or regret.

The hum of disco music filled the air as multicolored lights spun around the roller rink, casting vibrant patterns on the polished floor. Isaac laced up his roller skates, sneaking a glance at Penelope, who was tying hers with practiced ease. She looked effortlessly radiant under the flashing lights, her hair catching hints of neon as she laughed at his slightly nervous expression.

"You look like you've never skated before," Penelope teased, offering her hand as she stood up.

Isaac scoffed lightly, standing and wobbling a little for dramatic effect. "I'm a natural at everything I do. You, on the other hand, better watch out. I hear ballet doesn't translate to roller skating."

She smirked, a challenge sparkling in her eyes. "Let's see who survives the night, then."

The two of them wobbled onto the rink, Penelope gliding effortlessly while Isaac fumbled for balance, his long limbs flailing comically. "I feel like a baby deer," he muttered, gripping the railing.

"You look like one, too," Penelope said with a giggle, skating backwards to face him. "Loosen up, Isaac. Just feel the rhythm of the music."

As the upbeat disco track reverberated around them, Isaac took a deep breath and let go of the railing. Penelope's encouragement and infectious laughter gave him the push he needed. Slowly, he found his footing, or rather, his wheels, and managed to glide forward without looking entirely ridiculous.

"Look at that! You're doing it!" Penelope cheered, holding out her hand to him. "See? I knew you could!"

Isaac grabbed her hand, smiling at her excitement, but the moment was short lived. As Penelope tried to spin around gracefully, her skate caught on a bump, and she stumbled. In her attempt to regain balance, she swung her elbow out and it connected directly with Isaac's nose.

"Shit!" Isaac exclaimed, clutching his face as he stumbled back.

"Oh no!" Penelope gasped, immediately skating to his side. "Isaac, I'm so sorry! Are you okay?"

He pulled his hand away, revealing blood trickling from his nose. "Well," he said with a crooked smile, "that's one way to leave an impression."

Penelope winced but couldn't help laughing. "Come on, let's get you some ice before I break anything else."

They shuffled to a quieter, dimly lit corner of the rink, where Penelope fussed over Isaac with a bag of ice she'd charmed out of a concession stand worker. He leaned back on a cushioned bench, pressing the ice to his nose while Penelope sat cross-legged beside him.

"I really am sorry," she murmured, biting her lip as she looked at him. "I didn't mean to ruin our night."

Isaac waved her off, his voice muffled by the ice pack. "You didn't ruin anything. This will just make for a memorable story."

Penelope smiled shyly, her fingers playing with the hem of her sleeve. "You're being a good sport about it."

"I have to be," Isaac said, lowering the ice pack to reveal a slightly bruised nose and a lopsided grin. "I can't have the girl I fancied in ballet class thinking I'm a whiner."

Penelope blinked in surprise, her cheeks flushing. "You fancied me? Back then?"

"Of course I did," Isaac said, a warm chuckle escaping him. "I was only there because of you."

Penelope tilted her head, her voice soft. "All the girls were smitten with you, they wanted to dance with the sad boy who was far too good for the rest of them."

"Good?" Isaac laughed. "I think 'protege' was the word Miss Elena used."

Penelope giggled, shaking her head. "So humble."

"I am a pauper compared to the poorest man."

Penelope wiped at a slight trickle of blood remaining on Isaac's lip. "Well, you're the richest pauper I know, then!"

"You've been speaking too much with Anthony again." Isaac laughed.

"Your money doesn't matter to me, Isaac." Penelope shrugged. "It never was, there is so much to your heart than the money in your pocket. But you were missed when you left the company. Anthony missed seeing you there, I missed seeing you, too."

Isaac's smile softened as he gazed at her, a strand of her hair falling into her face. Without thinking, he reached out and gently tucked it behind her ear. Penelope froze for a moment, her breath catching as his fingers brushed her cheek.

"Can I kiss you?" Isaac asked quietly, his voice steady but filled with a vulnerability that made Penelope's heart skip a beat.

Her blush deepened, but she gave a small nod, her eyes meeting his. "Yeah," she whispered.

Isaac leaned in, his hand still lightly resting against her cheek as their lips met. The kiss was slow and sweet, the chaos of the rink fading into the background. It felt like the culmination of something unspoken, years of missed moments and quiet admiration coming to life in that single, tender connection.

After their kiss, the world around Isaac and Penelope seemed to blur, the pulsing lights of the roller disco dimming in their significance. For a moment, it was just them, locked in a quiet, unspoken connection. Penelope pulled back slightly, her cheeks flushed, her lips quirking into a shy, radiant smile.

"You're better at that than roller skating," she teased softly, her voice trembling with a mix of humor and lingering nerves.

Isaac chuckled, "Good to know my talents aren't entirely wasted tonight."

They sat there for a beat longer, the thrum of distant disco music filling the silence between them. Penelope's fingers idly traced the edge of the ice pack now resting on Isaac's hand.

"You're not mad about your nose, are you?" she asked, her brows knitting together with concern.

"Mad?" Isaac smirked, leaning slightly closer. "You've got to work a lot harder than that to scare me off."

Penelope rolled her eyes but couldn't suppress the grin tugging at her lips. "I don't know... I have a few more tricks up my sleeve."

Isaac leaned back, pretending to look cautious. "Should I be worried?"

"Only if you keep standing in the way of my elbows," she quipped, her laughter breaking the tension.

The two eventually returned to the main floor, though they opted to stay off the skates for the rest of the evening. Instead, they watched other couples glide across the rink, the kaleidoscope of lights reflecting in Penelope's warm eyes.

Isaac found himself captivated, not by the disco or the music, but by her. Every laugh, her easy humor, and the way she tilted her head as if absorbing every moment fully.

As the night wound down, they made their way outside, the chilly London air nipping at their skin. Isaac draped his jacket over Penelope's shoulders as they walked, the energy between them humming with something new, something unspoken but understood.

"Thank you for tonight," she said as they neared the bus stop. "It was... perfect. Well, except for the part where I almost broke your nose."

"Details," Isaac replied with a shrug. "Best date I've ever had."

She stopped walking, turning to face him. "Is that true?"

Isaac's expression softened, his green eyes meeting hers. "Absolutely."

Penelope smiled, slipping her hand into his. They didn't speak after that, letting the quiet of the city night surround them. It wasn't until the bus pulled up that Penelope squeezed his hand, her grip lingering as she stepped onto the platform.

"Next time," she called over her shoulder, "you'd better watch out for my skating skills. I'm dangerous, remember?"

"Dangerous and unforgettable," Isaac called back with a grin.

4

The flat was unusually quiet that evening, save for the low hum of a distant radio and the occasional creak of the old wooden floor. Isaac sat sprawled on the couch, flipping absentmindedly through a tattered book he'd promised himself he'd read but never really did. His nose, still sporting a faint bruise from the roller disco mishap, throbbed slightly when he scrunched it in thought.

Malcom emerged from the kitchen, mug in hand, and leaned against the doorway, his sharp eyes taking in Isaac's face. He smirked knowingly.

"What happened to you? Run into a wall? Or did the wall run into you?"

Isaac shot him a look, setting the book down. "Penelope. Roller disco. Long story," he said, trying to sound casual, but the faint smile tugging at his lips gave him away.

"Penelope," Malcom repeated, his tone light but his eyes thoughtful. He crossed the room, sitting in the chair opposite Isaac. "You've been spending a lot of time with her lately."

Isaac nodded, leaning back against the couch. "I have. And it's been... good. Really good, actually."

Malcom studied him for a moment, his usual teasing demeanor replaced with something gentler. "You fancy her," he said, not as a question but as a statement.

Isaac met his gaze, his confidence unshaken. "I love her."

Malcom blinked, surprised by the directness. "Love?"

"Yeah," Isaac said, sitting up straighter. "I know how it sounds, but it's true. I've never felt like this before. When I'm with her, it's like everything makes sense, you know? She's smart and funny, and... she sees me, Mal. Like really sees me."

Malcom didn't respond immediately. He just watched Isaac, his expression a mix of concern and something softer, almost protective. Then, without a word, he leaned forward, reaching into the side pocket of the armchair. When he sat back, he held a small orange pill bottle in his hand, the same one Isaac thought he'd hidden well.

Isaac froze.

"Mal..."

"I found it while I was cleaning," Malcom said, his voice calm but firm. He turned the bottle over in his hands, his thumb tracing the faded label. "It's nearly empty, Isaac."

Isaac's stomach twisted, his earlier confidence crumbling. He looked away, unable to meet Malcom's eyes.

"I can explain," he started, but Malcom cut him off gently.

"I'm not mad," Malcom said, leaning forward, his tone careful. "I just... I'm worried about you. This isn't you, mate. Or at least, it wasn't."

Isaac exhaled shakily, running a hand through his hair. "I don't need them," he said, though he didn't sound convinced. "It's just… things get overwhelming sometimes. The nightmares, the pressure, everything with Penelope…"

"Everything with Penelope?" Malcom prompted, his brow furrowing.

Isaac hesitated, the words catching in his throat. "I don't want to screw this up," he admitted quietly. "She means so much to me, and I'm terrified I'm going to ruin it somehow."

Malcom softened at that, setting the pill bottle down on the coffee table between them. "Isaac," he said, his voice steady, "you don't need these to be good for her. You don't need them to be enough. You already are."

Isaac's throat tightened, the weight of Malcom's words pressing against the knot of fear and guilt he carried.

"What if I'm not?" he whispered.

Malcom leaned back, crossing his arms. "Then you work at it. And you let people help you. Me, Penelope, Anthony. But you don't fix it with this," he said, nodding toward the bottle. "Not anymore."

For a long moment, the room was silent. Isaac stared at the bottle, his mind racing. Finally, he reached out and picked it up, weighing it in his hand. Then, with a deep breath, he stood and walked to the kitchen.

Malcom watched as Isaac opened the rubbish bin and dropped the bottle inside. When he turned back, there was a flicker of something lighter in his expression, though his eyes were still shadowed with uncertainty.

"Happy now?" Isaac asked, forcing a weak grin.

Malcom smiled, standing and clapping a hand on Isaac's shoulder. "Getting there. One step at a time, yeah?"

Isaac nodded, a faint sense of anxiety settling over him.

"I have class this afternoon," Malcom stated, beginning to gather his bag. Malcom was attending the university for medical, wanting to become a nurse. Isaac watched him carefully. "Will you be alright until I get back? We can have dinner at the pub."

"Yeah, I will be fine here." Isaac ran his hand through his unkempt hair, eyeing the guitar sitting near the couch. "I will be practicing the sheet music Anthony brought over."

Malcom grinned, raising a fist to signal rock, "*Jacked Pistols*!"

Isaac gave a similar sign, watching Malcom turn to leave. Isaac waited until he heard the steps racing down the path, when his eyes darted to the trash bin. He shook himself, turning to the couch to take up his guitar. Feeling the heavy metal strings whir beneath his fingertips. Anxiety crept along his spine, thought began to jumble as his mind raced.

Jumping to his feet, Isaac set his guitar aside, dashing across the room to the kitchen, opening the bin to retrieve the pill bottle. Opening the lid he dumped the pills out into his palm, discarding the bottle. Glaring hard at the white pills, Isaac trembled, his mouth watering as he began to sweat.

Popping all of the pills in his mouth, Isaac swallowed them dryly. Rushing to the sink to swallow mouthfuls of water to wash away the astrid bitter taste. He hissed, grasping the sink. Unable to process the thought as realization gripped tightly through his body. Isaac collapsed to his knees, a tear slipping down his cheek. He wiped it away bitterly, before more began to emerge. Weeping openly, shaking with agony as he began to feel the fizzled edges of his thoughts dull with such ferocity it nearly took his breath away.

Pulling himself to his feet, Isaac swayed momentarily, his vision tilting as he steadied himself. The sight of the rubbish still lingered in his mind, a bitter symbol of his struggle, and he couldn't bear to stay in the flat another second. Grabbing his jacket, he stepped out into the street, the cold evening air biting at his skin. It shocked his senses awake, a clarity he hadn't felt all day.

Without a clear plan, he began to jog, his limbs protesting with every step. The chill seeped through his clothes, numbing him as he pushed forward, deeper into the city. The rhythmic pounding of his feet against the pavement matched the chaos in his mind, and it wasn't until his lungs burned and his legs screamed for rest that he slowed, panting heavily.

The shops on either side glowed softly in the early evening, and a familiar neon sign caught his eye. The club, one he'd been to once with Anthony. The memories of that night felt distant, wrapped in a haze of nostalgia and regret. Without hesitation, he made his way toward it, the promise of music and distraction too tempting to resist.

Inside, the dimly lit entrance felt like a world apart. Isaac fumbled to show his ID, but the doorman waved him through with an indifferent nod. The moment he stepped past the threshold, the music hit him like a wave. The pulsing bass reverberated through his chest, the vibrations drowning out the noise in his head. He stood still for a moment, awash in the kaleidoscope of lights that danced across the room, colors cascading like liquid over a shimmering wall of trickling water nearby.

"Feeling alright?"

The voice was smooth and rich, cutting through the noise with practiced ease. Isaac turned, his eyes meeting those of a man with deep black eyes and dark skin that seemed to glow under the vibrant hues of pinks and greens. His close-shaved fade gleamed in the shifting light, and his smile was warm, inviting.

Isaac swallowed hard, his body buzzing with a mixture of nerves and something else he couldn't quite name. "Yeah," he said, his voice louder than he intended over the music. "Just... feeling it."

The man's smile widened, a knowing glint in his eyes. "I feel that," he echoed, nodding along to the beat. "Wanna dance?"

Isaac hesitated for only a moment before nodding. The idea of movement, of losing himself in the rhythm, was irresistible. He followed the man onto the dance floor, the crowd swallowing them in a sea of bodies that moved like a living organism, swaying and shifting with the music.

The rhythm took over, and Isaac let himself go. His limbs moved to the beat, his mind surrendering to the pulse of the bass. It was freeing, the closest thing to peace he'd felt in days. Around him, the bodies seemed to ebb and flow like waves, and he became part of the current, his own body responding in kind.

Warm hands found his hips, sliding up with a gentle pressure that sent a spark through him. The touch drew him closer, pulling him into the rhythm of another body. Isaac didn't resist. He turned his head slightly, catching the man's knowing smile through the haze of light and shadow.

The music drowned out his thoughts, the thrum of the bass replacing the pounding of his heart. For a moment, the weight of everything, his nightmares, his fears, his constant battle with himself, faded away. All that remained was the beat, the warmth of another human's touch, and the unspoken promise of escape in the movement of their bodies.

The song shifted into a slower, deeper rhythm, the bass a steady throb that seemed to reverberate through the floor and up into Isaac's chest. The hands on his hips lingered, their pressure gentle but insistent, pulling him closer until there was barely any space between their bodies. Isaac's breath hitched, his eyes darting upward to meet the man's gaze.

"You've got moves," the man said, his voice pitched low, just loud enough to be heard over the music. His smile was warm, teasing, and Isaac felt a flush rise to his cheeks. Flashing a mischievous smile and motioning for Isaac to follow. Hesitation flickered for a moment, but the pull of curiosity and the promise of distraction were too strong to resist.

They moved away from the packed dance floor, slipping into a hallway illuminated by pulsing neon lights. It was quieter here, the music muffled but still present, a steady pulse in the background. The man pushed open a door, revealing a small back room with a low couch, a table scattered with empty glasses, and the faint scent of smoke clinging to the air.

Isaac hesitated in the doorway, his fingers brushing against the frame. "Are we allowed back here?"

The man chuckled, stepping closer. "What they don't know won't hurt them." His voice was smooth, coaxing.

Isaac stepped inside, letting the door fall shut behind him. The man settled on the couch, patting the cushion beside him. Isaac joined him, his heart pounding in his chest, though whether from nerves or anticipation, he couldn't say.

"You're tense," the man observed, his dark eyes searching Isaac's face. "You need to let go a little."

Before Isaac could respond, the man leaned in, his hand resting lightly on Isaac's knee. The room felt smaller, the air heavier, and Isaac's breath caught in his throat. The strong hand massaging through the layer of ripped denim. Hot mouth kissing up the length of his exposed neck. Drawing a moan from Isaac's lips.

Then, just as the man's hand began to slide upward, the door burst open.

"Isaac?"

Malcom's voice cut through the moment like a knife. Isaac jerked away, nearly tumbling off the couch as he turned to see Malcom standing in the doorway, his expression a mix of confusion and concern.

The man leaned back, his brows raising in surprise but not much else. "He your boyfriend?" he asked, his tone amused.

Isaac scrambled to his feet, his cheeks flushing with embarrassment. "Malcom, what—what are you doing here?"

"I could ask you the same thing," Malcom replied, stepping fully into the room. His eyes flicked between Isaac and the man, lingering for a moment on their proximity before landing back on Isaac. "I went back to the flat. I saw you run off, it took a while to figure out where you had run off too."

Isaac's stomach twisted. Of course, Malcom had followed him.

The man rose from the couch, brushing imaginary lint from his shirt. "Well, looks like your evening just got more complicated," he said, flashing a sly smile at Isaac before turning to Malcom. "Nice to meet you, mate."

Malcom didn't return the sentiment, his gaze fixed firmly on Isaac.

"I—I should go," Isaac stammered, stepping toward Malcom. The man shrugged, clearly unbothered, and sank back onto the couch as if nothing had happened.

Once they were out in the alleyway behind the club, Malcom grabbed Isaac's arm, pulling him to a stop. "What the hell was that?"

"It was nothing," Isaac said quickly, though his voice betrayed his unease.

"Nothing?" Malcolm's brow furrowed, his grip tightening slightly. "You were in the back room of a club with some random guy. What are you doing, Isaac?"

Isaac pulled free, his frustration bubbling to the surface. "I'm trying to forget, okay? Just for one bloody night."

Malcolm's expression softened, the anger in his eyes giving way to concern. "Forget what?"

Isaac hesitated, his chest tightening. "Everything. The nightmares, the pills." His voice cracked on the last word, and he looked away, unable to meet Malcom's gaze.

Malcom exhaled. "Isaac... you don't have to do this alone. You don't have to spiral."

Isaac laughed bitterly, shaking his head. "What choice do I have, Malcolm? It's not like you're exactly lining up to help."

Malcolm flinched, the words hitting harder than Isaac intended. But he didn't deny them. Instead, he reached into his pocket and pulled out the familiar pill bottle, holding it up between them.

"You need to stop this," Malcom said quietly, his voice steady but firm. "Before it stops you. If Neil found out…"

"He won't."

Malcom sighed heavily. "You took the rest of them…you know what that could have done to you."

Isaac stared at the bottle, the weight of Malcom's words pressing down on him like a heavy stone. "It wasn't enough to cause so much damage."

"That is the mentality of an addict," Malcom hissed, clutching tightly to the empty bottle in his hands. "Your choices don't affect just yourself, Isaac. Fucking with some random guy in a club won't build love and trust with her, would it, Isaac? It would ruin her to learn about this…"

Isaac gulped, his eyes filled with tears. Malcom was the only one who ever saw him this way, who understood the torment he felt. As always, Malcom was right.

Finally, Malcolm placed the bottle back in his pocket. "Let's get out of here," he said, his tone softer now. "We'll talk. Properly."

Isaac nodded, his throat too tight to speak. As they stepped back into the cool night air, the weight of what he'd nearly done settled over him like a blanket, suffocating and inescapable.

5

The morning air was sharp, biting at the edges of Isaac's lungs as he and Anthony made their way through Hyde Park. The brisk cold made their breaths visible, a smoky mist that lingered in the chill. The trees were bare, skeletal branches reaching up into a pale, clear sky, and the park was almost empty this early on a Sunday, just a few joggers, walkers, and the occasional cyclist weaving through the paths.

Isaac ran with his hands thrust deep into the pockets of his hoodie, trying to keep the trembling in his fingers from showing. Every step felt like dragging his body through mud, the exhaustion in his bones deeper than usual. Maybe it was the nightmares last night, or the ever-present anxiety gnawing at the edges of his mind. His nose is sore from the brutal elbow he received from Penelope.

Anthony, however, seemed oblivious to Isaac's inner turmoil as they fell into step with each other. He was always the more chipper of the two, a grin playing at his lips as he spoke animatedly about plans for the band. "So, Neil's on board with us using the theatre a few nights a week to practice," Anthony said, his breath puffing out in front of him like clouds of steam. "Think it's a good move, right?"

"Yeah, yeah, it's good," Isaac replied, his voice quieter than he intended. The idea of playing music again was appealing. He focused on keeping his breathing steady, matching his pace with Anthony's.

There was a stretch of silence between them as they rounded a corner, Isaac watching the people around them, the rhythm of their footsteps synchronizing with his own.

Anthony cleared his throat eventually, glancing sidelong at Isaac. "How's Penelope?"

Isaac's heart skipped a beat at the question. It was unexpected. Normally, they ran in silence, the rhythm of their breathing and the sound of their feet hitting the ground enough to fill the gaps in conversation. But today, Anthony wanted to talk. "Uh, good," Isaac replied, trying to keep his tone nonchalant. "We've been hanging out more."

"Yeah?" Anthony's gaze lingered on Isaac for a moment too long, his brow furrowing slightly. "You guys... getting closer?"

Isaac felt his cheeks heat up, the blush creeping up his neck. "I guess," he muttered, his fingers numb from the cold.

"Feels weird, huh?" Anthony remarked, his voice light, but there was an edge to it, a seriousness that made Isaac's stomach twist. "I mean, considering..."

"Yeah, it does," Isaac said, his breath catching as he tried to keep his voice steady. "Feels weird for me too."

Anthony nodded, keeping his eyes fixed on the path ahead. "You know, you didn't have to break it off, Isaac," he said quietly, his voice soft and careful. "We could've worked through it."

Isaac's heart clenched at the reminder, in the past he couldn't escape, no matter how far he ran. "I had to," he replied, his voice barely a whisper. "It wasn't... it wasn't right, Anthony."

"Because of my faith," Anthony said, the words almost a question. "You're not angry with me?"

Isaac shook his head, feeling the weight of it all settle in his chest. "No. I'm not. I know how devout a Catholic you are...there are more important things to consider."

Anthony's gaze softened, his lips twitching as if he wanted to smile but didn't quite let himself. "I wish I could have loved you the way you deserve."

"You're still one of my best mates," Isaac said, swallowing past the lump in his throat. "It's enough."

Anthony slowed his pace, coming to a stop and turning to face Isaac. "Is it?"

Isaac stopped as well, the cold air biting at his cheeks. He hesitated for a moment, then took a deep breath. "I still love you, Anthony," he admitted, his eyes meeting Anthony's. "I can't just... turn it off."

Anthony's expression was a mix of sadness and longing. "I wish I could, Isaac. I do. But—"

"Your faith," Isaac finished for him, his voice cracking. "It's more important to you than—"

"Than us," Anthony cut in, his voice breaking slightly. "Yeah."

Isaac looked away, his heart pounding. He wanted to tell Anthony it didn't have to be that way, that they could find a way to be together despite it all, but he knew better than to hope for that. "I'm trying to... find a way to move on," he said quietly, his breath fogging in front of him. "Perhaps I can, with Penelope."

"She could be good for you," Anthony said after a moment, his tone gentle. "She makes you smile in ways I can't. She could give you the love you need."

"Yeah," Isaac replied, feeling a pang in his chest. "Maybe I need that right now."

Anthony nodded, as if understanding. "You should ask her out more often," he suggested, his voice encouraging. "Show her you're serious. Not just chips and flirting."

Isaac smiled, a real one, if only for a moment. "I think I will."

"Good," Anthony said, clapping Isaac on the shoulder. "But be careful how you treat my sister. I can still kick your ass."

Isaac laughed. "You could try."

6

The evening air in London buzzed with life as Isaac led Penelope through winding streets, their pace quickening with excitement. She glanced at him curiously, her brows lifting.

"Where are we going, exactly?" Penelope asked, tucking a stray curl behind her ear.

"You'll see," Isaac replied with a sly grin, his eyes sparkling under the glow of the streetlights. "Just trust me."

They turned a corner and arrived at a lively club, its marquee flashing Improv Dance Night in bold neon letters. Penelope froze, her lips parting in surprise.

"An improv dance club? Are you serious?" she asked, though her smile betrayed her amusement.

"Completely serious," Isaac said, holding the door open for her. "Come on, it'll be fun."

Inside, the club buzzed with an energy that seemed to seep into the very walls. The air was alive with the rhythm of the music, each beat reverberating through the floor like a heartbeat. Shifting colored lights danced across the stage, casting vibrant hues of blue, pink, and gold over the crowd. The DJ, stationed high above the dance floor, expertly wove melodies into a pulsing symphony that made the atmosphere feel electric.

Clusters of dancers gathered around the edges of the room—some stretching with focused determination, others laughing and exchanging animated chatter. Isaac glanced at Penelope, her eyes wide with curiosity as she took in the scene.

"Alright," he said, a smile tugging at his lips, "first things first—let's get drinks."

He reached for her hand, and she let him guide her toward the bar. The contact was brief, but it sent a spark through him, a warmth that lingered even after he let go.

As they sipped their drinks and talked, the energy in the room seemed to swell. The music shifted to something faster, sharper, and the chatter of the crowd dimmed slightly as a spotlight snapped onto the stage.

A figure emerged—a lively emcee, dressed in a sequined jacket that shimmered under the lights. Grabbing a microphone, their voice boomed over the sound system, instantly commanding attention.

"Alright, everyone, it's time for the moment you've been waiting for! Freestyle dance battle!" The crowd erupted into cheers and applause as the emcee grinned, holding up their hand for quiet.

"And now," they continued, scanning the room theatrically, "who's ready to show us some moves? Let's see... you!" The emcee pointed directly at Isaac, who blinked in surprise. "And... you!" Their finger shifted to Penelope.

Isaac turned to her with a playful shrug, his grin widening. "Guess we're up."

Penelope laughed, shaking her head in mock exasperation. "You planned this, didn't you?"

"Not this time," Isaac said, holding out his hand once more. "But I'm not about to say no."

Taking his hand, Penelope let herself be led toward the stage, her laughter mixing with the crowd's cheers as they climbed the steps together. The spotlight followed them, casting their intertwined hands in brilliant light as the DJ cued up a new track. The bass dropped, and the room came alive with anticipation.

Isaac stepped forward, his movements fluid and confident as he rolled his shoulders and fell into rhythm with the beat. Penelope followed suit, her natural grace lighting up the stage. They mirrored each other, their bodies swaying and spinning in a playful, synchronized exchange.

The energy shifted as Isaac moved closer, extending a hand to her. "Shall we?"

Penelope took it with a coy smile. "Try to keep up."

Their flirtation played out in every step—an exaggerated dip that left Penelope giggling, a teasing shimmy from Isaac that made her roll her eyes but laugh anyway. The crowd cheered louder with every turn and flourished.

As the song ended, they struck a final pose, breathless and beaming. The room erupted in applause, and Penelope turned to Isaac, shaking her head in disbelief.

"That was incredible," she said as they stepped off the stage.

"You were incredible," Isaac corrected, his grin widening.

As they stepped out of the club, the cool night air wrapped around them like a refreshing balm, a sharp contrast to the sweltering energy they'd left behind. Penelope bumped Isaac's shoulder playfully, her laughter light and breathless. "So," she teased, "is that your secret weapon? Luring unsuspecting women to dance clubs and then sweeping them off their feet?"

Isaac chuckled, shoving his hands into his jacket pockets. "You caught me," he said, tilting his head toward her. "Though I can't say it's ever worked out this well before."

Penelope rolled her eyes but couldn't suppress a smile. "Well, it was either that or you've been practicing solo routines in secret."

"Maybe," he replied, his voice teasing. "Or maybe I just had the perfect partner tonight."

She nudged him again, her cheeks pink under the glow of the streetlights. "Are you ever going to stop pretending you're done with dancing? Because that performance says otherwise."

Isaac chuckled, tucking his hands deep into his jacket pockets. "I don't know, Pen. It's... complicated."

Penelope nudged him gently with her elbow, her voice soft but insistent. "It doesn't have to be," she said, her gaze searching his. "You're good at it, Isaac. Really good. You should think about it."

He didn't answer right away, his footsteps slowing slightly as his eyes traced the uneven cracks in the pavement. The streetlights cast a faint glow around them, their long shadows stretching across the sidewalk.

"I just..." he began, then stopped, shaking his head. "It's not that simple."

Penelope tilted her head, watching him closely. "What's holding you back?" she asked gently, her tone free of judgment.

Isaac exhaled a long breath, his lips curving into a faint, almost self-deprecating smile. "Maybe it's easier to convince myself I don't belong on a stage anymore than to face the possibility I never really did."

Penelope stopped walking, forcing him to pause and meet her gaze. "That's rubbish, and you know it," she said firmly. "You belong, Isaac. More than most. The way you move? The way you feel the music? It's not just talent—it's passion. And that's rare."

Her words hung in the air between them, the chill of the night contrasting with the warmth of her conviction. Isaac held her gaze for a moment before looking away, his hands tightening in his pockets.

"Come on, I'll walk you home."

They arrived at her building, the light in the front window casting a warm glow over the street. Penelope turned to him, her expression tender.

"Thanks for tonight," she said, her voice barely above a whisper. "It was... perfect."

Before he could reply, she leaned in, her lips brushing his in a kiss that was soft and full of unspoken promise.

When she pulled back, there was a glimmer of mischief in her eyes. "Come up?"

Isaac hesitated, his smile tinged with regret. "I wish I could, but my uncle's workshop starts early tomorrow. I need to help out."

Penelope tilted her head, studying him for a moment before nodding. "Okay. But don't make me wait too long for another night like this."

"Wouldn't dream of it," Isaac replied, stepping back reluctantly.

7

I saac climbed the stairs to Penelope's flat, his breath slightly visible in the crisp evening air. The takeaway bags swung in his hand, the aroma of spices and warmth escaping faintly from the folded edges. He shifted the bags to one hand, raising the other to knock on her door, but before his knuckles touched wood, it opened.

Penelope stood there in cozy, oversized pajamas—striped bottoms and a soft, off-the-shoulder sweater that hinted at her collarbone. Her hair was loosely tied back, with a few stray curls framing her face. She smiled, warm and easy, her eyes lighting up as she spotted the bags.

"You brought the good stuff, I hope," she teased, stepping aside to let him in.

Isaac held up the bags in mock seriousness. "Only the finest for a night of vintage cinema and questionable taste in takeout."

She laughed, closing the door behind him. The flat smelled faintly of vanilla candles and the herbal tea she'd set out on the coffee table. The room was softly lit by a single lamp in the corner, giving everything a golden hue. The couch was piled with mismatched cushions and a thick knit blanket, already beckoning him.

"Set it up over there," Penelope said, nodding toward the coffee table as she grabbed plates from the kitchen. Isaac obeyed, laying out the food while stealing glances at her as she bustled around.

A few minutes later, they were settled in, cartons open, chopsticks in hand, as the old black-and-white film flickered to life on the TV. The movie's grainy quality and dramatic music filled the small space, but Isaac found his focus drifting more toward Penelope than the screen.

As the movie played on, Penelope leaned into his side, resting her head against his shoulder. The soft pressure felt natural, like pieces clicking into place. Isaac froze for a moment, unsure if he should move or say something, but Penelope's contented sigh melted his hesitation. He relaxed, draping his arm lightly along the back of the couch, close but not touching her.

Her hand moved then, trailing along his forearm, her fingers brushing the fabric of his shirt with the gentlest pressure. It wasn't demanding or overt, just a quiet, intimate gesture. Isaac felt his heartbeat quicken, his pulse pounding in his ears louder than the dialogue from the screen.

He glanced down at her. Penelope was already looking up at him, her eyes searching his face, a small, tentative smile playing on her lips.

"Hi," she whispered, her voice low and sweet, as though they weren't already sharing the same space, the same breath.

Isaac swallowed hard, a nervous chuckle escaping him. "Hi," he echoed, his voice slightly shaky.

Penelope shifted, sitting up just enough to meet his gaze fully. Her hand slid up to his shoulder, steadying herself as she leaned closer.

Isaac felt the warmth of her breath before their lips met, soft and tentative at first, a question neither needed to ask aloud.

Isaac's free hand slid around Penelope's waist, guiding her closer as if their bodies were magnets, the pull inevitable. Her fingers curled against the fabric of his collar, tugging him slightly forward as if she couldn't bear the space between them. Their kiss, initially soft and exploratory, grew deeper, more assured, like the slow crescendo of a song. Each movement of their lips felt deliberate, a shared language spoken without words.

When they finally paused, their foreheads touched, their breaths mingling in the intimate quiet between them. Penelope's lips, still slightly parted, brushed his as she murmured, "Perfect."

Isaac managed a breathless chuckle, his voice hoarse as he replied, "Yeah. Perfect."

A gentle smile curved her lips before she shifted her weight, and before Isaac fully processed it, Penelope maneuvered herself to straddle his thighs. The sudden proximity sent a shockwave through him; her warmth pressed against him, her fingers grazing the nape of his neck before tangling in his hair.

Her laugh was low and teasing, a melodic sound that danced over his skin. "Too fast?" she asked, her lips reddened and slightly swollen.

Isaac's hands, now firmly settled on the curve of her hips, tightened instinctively. He shook his head, his pulse thrumming wildly. "I'd gladly take you, Pen," he said, voice thick with want, "but wouldn't this complicate your vow to the church?"

Her response was immediate—a mischievous grin followed by her lips crashing into his again. "It's not my first time, Isaac," she whispered between kisses, her breath hot against his cheek.

Isaac groaned, his hands sliding down to grip her thighs, pulling her closer, until Penelope abruptly pulled back, her brow raised, a glint of curiosity in her dark eyes. "You're not a virgin, are you?"

The question caught him off guard, and he laughed—a deep, amused sound. "No."

"Good." She leaned in, her lips grazing his as her hands slid through his hair, nails teasing his scalp. Her playful tug drew a low growl from his throat, and she pulled back, her gaze bright with challenge. "Do you have experience with women?"

A smirk spread across his face as he caught her hand and pressed a slow kiss to her palm. "Don't believe all the rumors, Pen. I know my way around."

Her laugh turned into a yelp of surprise as Isaac moved swiftly, flipping their positions. Now kneeling on the floor, he hovered over her as she leaned back against the couch. Her dark hair spilled out of its tie, cascading over the cushions like a frame for her wide eyed expression. Her sweater had shifted slightly, exposing one delicate shoulder, the curve of her collarbone catching the dim light.

Isaac dipped his head, his breath ghosting over her skin before his teeth grazed that exposed shoulder. A sharp inhale from Penelope rewarded him, the sound more intoxicating than any drink.

Her eyes darkened as she let out a soft, pleased hiss. "Careful, Isaac," she murmured, her fingers tracing down the line of his jaw. "You're playing with fire."

He chuckled, his voice low and gravelly, his lips brushing against her skin again. "Good thing I've never been afraid of a little heat." Pulling the sweater aside to kiss the tender skin of her breast. Penelope sighed, her hands finding the fall of his hair to pull him closer.

"Oh, you're good," she whispered.

Isaac paused, his lips hovering just above her collarbone, his breath warm against her skin. He glanced up at her, a playful glint in his eye as a crooked smile tugged at his lips.

"You just noticed that now?" he teased, his voice low and rich, filled with a confidence that sent a shiver down her spine.

Penelope's laugh was soft, almost breathless, as her fingers trailed over his shoulders, brushing against the back of his neck. "Maybe I like pretending to be surprised," she murmured, her voice carrying the same teasing edge.

Isaac shifted, pressing a kiss to her neck, then her jawline, each touch deliberate and maddeningly slow. "And here I thought you were the honest type," he muttered against her skin, his lips brushing her ear.

Her fingers tightened in his hair, tugging just enough to draw a gasp from him. "I never said I wasn't honest," she countered, her grin devilish as she met his gaze, their faces mere inches apart. "I just didn't know you'd be this good."

Isaac laughed, the sound vibrating through her as his hands found their way back to her waist. "Careful, Pen. Flattery might get you everywhere."

Her response was immediate and bold. She tugged him closer, her lips finding him in a kiss that was no longer playful but heated and demanding, her movements filled with a quiet confidence that matched his own.

As their connection deepened, the forgotten movie played on, the flickering black and white images casting dancing shadows across the room. The world outside seemed to dissolve, leaving only the two of them caught in a moment that felt endless.

When they finally pulled apart, both of them were breathing heavily, their faces still close. Penelope's lips curved into a satisfied smile. "I think you might've just ruined black and white movies for me. Not sure I'll be able to concentrate on one again."

Isaac chuckled, brushing a strand of hair from her face. "Guess we'll just have to find a new way to pass the time, then."

She raised an eyebrow, her fingers tracing idle patterns along his jawline. "I'm sure we'll think of something."

Isaac's lips trailed lower, his movements deliberate and tender, leaving a line of warm kisses along her stomach just below her navel. Penelope's breath hitched, her fingers curling instinctively into the fabric of the couch beneath her. His hands rested on her thighs, his touch gentle but firm, grounding them both in the moment.

She arched slightly under his touch, the soft fabric of her pajama bottoms brushing against his palms as he hooked his fingers at the waistband, hesitating only briefly to meet her gaze. Penelope's eyes were warm, filled with trust and anticipation, and she gave a small nod, her lips curving into a faint smile.

Isaac eased the material down slowly, revealing the delicate silk of her knickers with a tiny red bow that made him chuckle softly. "You're full of surprises," he murmured, his voice carrying a teasing warmth that made her laugh.

"Glad you noticed," she replied, her tone light but edged with the same desire that had his heart racing.

He shifted to remove her pajama bottoms completely, his movements reverent as if unwrapping something precious. When her bare foot brushed against his chest playfully, he caught her ankle gently, his fingers tracing along the smooth curve before pressing a kiss to the inside of her ankle.

Penelope smirked, extending her leg, her flexibility effortless as she rested it on his shoulder. "You really know how to take your time," she teased, her voice soft but laced with amusement.

Isaac smiled, leaning forward to press a kiss to her calf, then her thigh. "I like to savor the moment," he said, his tone earnest. His hands caressed her hips, his thumbs brushing over her skin as he dipped his head, his lips trailing just above the curve of her waist.

"Don't keep a girl waiting, Isaac," she whispered, her tone a mix of playfulness and longing.

"Never dream of it," he said, his voice low and steady. Pressing his mouth to the fabric of her knickers. Biting the little red bow, hearing Penelope laugh above him.

She was warm, tasting of sweetness and silk. Isaac enjoyed the way she squirmed and sighed, pressing closer into her, tasting the depths of her. Losing himself to the moment, his head was held firmly in place by Penelope's thighs. Her fingers grasping deeply into the length of his hair, drawing him closer. The leg over his shoulder hooking him in, without release.

"Isaac," Penelope gasped, yanking his head back.

Isaac's gaze met hers, the intensity in his eyes mirroring the flush on her cheeks. Her breaths came quick and shallow, her lips parted as if searching for words that wouldn't come. He rested his chin on her knee, his hands sliding down to gently grip her hips, steadying her trembling frame.

"Everything alright?" he asked, his voice husky but laced with genuine concern.

Penelope nodded, her fingers loosening their grip in his hair. "More than alright," she murmured, her voice breathless, but there was a playful glint in her eye. She ran a hand down his cheek, her thumb brushing over his jawline.

Isaac chuckled, pressing a kiss to her knee before sitting back slightly, his palms still caressing the soft curve of her thighs. "You've got a way of making me lose track of everything," he admitted, his tone warm and teasing.

"Likewise," Penelope replied, her lips curving into a smile as she sat up straighter. She leaned forward, her hands trailing down his chest to rest against the waistband of his jeans, her touch light but deliberate. "But I think we both need this..."

8

The scent of rosin and faint perfume hung in the air as Isaac pushed open the double doors to the ballet studio. The space was cavernous, with high ceilings and walls lined with mirrors reflecting the warm glow of afternoon light streaming through large windows. Soft piano music filled the room, each delicate note underscoring the graceful movements of dancers scattered across the floor. Isaac adjusted his jacket, scanning the space until his eyes landed on Anthony, standing by the upright piano near the corner of the room.

Anthony looked up as Isaac approached, his posture stiffening slightly. There was an unspoken tension in the air, something Isaac couldn't quite place.

"Hey," Isaac greeted, offering a small smile.

Anthony nodded in return, glancing down at the piano keys before speaking. "What brings you here?"

"Picking Pen up," Isaac said, leaning casually against the piano. "She told me she'd be wrapping up around now."

Anthony's lips twitched, almost as if he wanted to smile but thought better of it. "You coming to the pub later? Open mic night. The boys are getting beers. Malcom's doing his thing again—probably murder a classic."

Isaac chuckled, though the slight edge in Anthony's tone didn't go unnoticed. "Yeah, I'll be there. Sounds like a good time."

Before Anthony could respond, a burst of laughter and excited chatter erupted from the far side of the room. Both men turned their heads to see a group of women gathered in a tight circle, their animated gestures and squeals filling the studio with an infectious energy. At the center of it all stood Penelope, her face alight with joy, clutching a piece of paper like it was the most precious thing in the world.

Anthony's gaze lingered on the group for a moment before he gave Isaac a pat on the shoulder. "See you at the pub," he said, his voice flat, before turning and walking away, leaving Isaac to watch him go with a furrowed brow.

Isaac shifted his focus back to Penelope, her laughter drawing him closer like a magnet. He crossed the studio, weaving through dancers packing up their bags and chatting in smaller clusters.

"What's all the excitement about?" he asked as he reached her, his voice warm despite the slight unease creeping into his chest.

Penelope turned to him, her eyes shining with exhilaration. "Isaac! Oh my gosh, you won't believe it." She held up the paper for him to see. "It's from New York—one of the biggest dance companies there. They accepted me! I got the contract!"

The words hit him like a punch to the gut, but Isaac kept his expression steady, his smile unwavering. "Pen, that's incredible," he said, pulling her into a hug. Her warmth against him was a cruel reminder of what he'd soon lose.

"It's everything I've worked for," she said, pulling back slightly to look at him. "Five years in New York—it's the dream."

"Five years," he repeated softly, nodding. "You're going to be amazing."

Penelope beamed, oblivious to the storm brewing behind his steady exterior.

"Want to go for a walk?" she asked. "I need to calm down a bit before I completely combust from excitement."

"Sure," he said, his voice steady.

The park near the studio was quiet, the faint rustle of leaves and the distant sound of children playing serving as a tranquil backdrop. Isaac bought two coffees from a small stall, handing one to Penelope as they strolled along the winding paths.

"I still can't believe it," Penelope said, her fingers curled around the warm cup. "This is what I've been dreaming of since I was a kid."

Isaac nodded, sipping his coffee. "You deserve it. You've worked harder than anyone I know."

She glanced at him, her expression softening in a way that made his heart ache. "But it's going to be hard, leaving everyone. Leaving you."

Isaac's grip tightened on his cup, but he plastered on a smile that didn't reach his eyes. "Hey, it's only five years. You'll blink, and it'll be over."

Penelope let out a soft laugh, the sound barely cutting through the tension hanging between them. "Easy for you to say," she murmured, nudging him with her elbow. "You're not the one moving halfway across the world."

"No," he replied, his voice low, "but I'll be here, cheering you on. Always."

She stopped walking, turning to face him under the faint glow of a street lamp. Her gaze was steady, her lips curved in a bittersweet smile. "Isaac, you can't wait for me."

The words landed like a blow, stealing the breath from his lungs. He blinked at her, trying to muster a response, but his throat felt too tight.

"I mean it," Penelope continued, stepping closer, her voice firm but gentle. "You have to promise me you won't. Five years is a long time, and it's not fair to either of us."

"It's not—" he began, but she cut him off, placing a hand on his arm.

"It is," she insisted, her thumb brushing lightly against his sleeve. "Five years is a lifetime, Isaac. You'll meet people, date... fall in love. I want you to live your life, not put it on hold for me."

He shook his head, a humorless laugh escaping him. "Pen, how can I even think about someone else when—"

"Promise me," she interrupted, her voice soft but unyielding. "If we're both single when I come back, we can... see where we are. Give it another crack. But until then, we have to move forward. Both of us."

Isaac searched her face, hoping to find some crack in her resolve, some hint that she didn't mean it. But her gaze held him with an earnestness that left no room for argument.

"Penelope," he said quietly, his voice breaking over her name.

"Promise me, Isaac," she whispered, her eyes glistening as she held his gaze.

He swallowed hard, feeling the weight of her words settle heavily on his chest. "I promise," he said finally, though every fiber of his being screamed against it.

Her lips trembled, but she smiled, nodding as if she believed him. "Good," she said softly, stepping closer to rest her head against his chest.

Isaac wrapped his arms around her, holding her tightly, as though it might keep her from slipping away. But the promise sat between them like a wall, an unyielding reminder that no matter how close they stood, she was already gone.

"Come on," she pulled away too soon. "We better get to the pub before Anthony kills us for being late."

The pub buzzed with life, its dim, golden light casting a warm glow over polished wooden tables and scuffed floorboards. The mingling scents of spilled beer, fried food, and a faint trace of smoke filled the air, blending seamlessly with the hum of chatter and bursts of laughter. In one corner, a man strummed a guitar on a small, makeshift stage, the gentle melody weaving through the din. The walls were cluttered with framed photos, old theater posters, and a mishmash of signs that gave the place a lived-in charm.

Isaac and Penelope stepped inside, the door creaking shut behind them as a gust of cool night air followed. Penelope's cheeks were still flushed from the brisk walk, her eyes sparkling with excitement as they found their way to a crowded table near the center of the room. Anthony and Malcom were already there, surrounded by a handful of others from the theater, their animated conversation punctuated by loud guffaws and the occasional clink of glasses.

"Finally!" Anthony called out, raising his pint in greeting. "Thought you two might've ditched us for a romantic moonlit stroll or something."

Isaac forced a grin, sliding into a seat beside Penelope. "Wouldn't miss Malcom's grand performance," he replied, nodding toward the stage.

"Careful, mate," Malcom shot back with a smirk, "you're in for a show you won't forget."

The banter flowed easily around the table, and Isaac played his part, laughing at Anthony's exaggerated stories and raising his glass when someone proposed a toast. Yet with each passing moment, the weight in his chest grew heavier, pressing against his ribs like a silent reminder of what loomed ahead.

Across from him, Penelope was radiant. Her laughter rang out like a melody, her hands animated as she recounted her news to the group. "Five years in New York," she said for the third time, shaking her head in disbelief. "I still can't believe it's real."

The table erupted in congratulations, and Anthony raised his glass. "To Penelope! The one who's too damn talented for the rest of us."

"Here, here!" Malcom added, thumping the table.

Isaac lifted his drink, forcing a smile as the others cheered.

Penelope's joy was infectious, lighting up the space around her like a warm fire on a cold night. But to Isaac, it only made the shadows inside him darker. Every word she spoke of New York, of her future, felt like a thread unraveling the fabric of a life they could together. And as her smile widened, he felt his own slipping away, no matter how tightly he tried to hold onto it.

At one point, Isaac excused himself quietly, slipping through the bustling pub and into the small, dimly lit bathroom. The muffled hum of laughter and conversation faded as the door swung shut behind him, leaving only the faint buzz of the overhead light and the dull rush of his heartbeat pounding in his ears.

He approached the sink and gripped its edges tightly, his knuckles whitening as he leaned forward to stare at his reflection. His face was pale, his jaw tight, his eyes shadowed with exhaustion and the weight of emotions he could no longer keep at bay. His chest felt impossibly tight, like a band was constricting around his lungs, and his mind spiraled, replaying Penelope's words over and over.

Five years.

The thought gnawed at him, tearing through his composure. His life without her stretched out like an endless void, a landscape of days she wouldn't fill. No laughter, no quiet moments in the park, no light teasing banter. It was unbearable.

His hand slipped into his jacket pocket, fumbling for the small container he kept hidden there. Pulling it out, he shook out a single pill, the faint rattle echoing in the silence of the room. His fingers trembled as he stared down at the tiny capsule resting in his palm, the weight of it disproportionate to its size.

Without hesitation, he placed it on his tongue and swallowed dry, his throat tightening as he fought against the rising tide of panic. He closed his eyes, waiting for the familiar numbness to seep in, dulling the sharp edges of his thoughts and quieting the ache that clawed at his chest.

The room felt colder now, or maybe it was him. He let out a shaky breath and turned on the tap, cupping cold water in his hands and splashing it onto his face. The shock of it grounded him, and he forced himself to take slow, measured breaths. Droplets clung to his eyelashes and dripped from his jaw as he straightened, staring at his reflection again.

His mask was back in place. The tightness in his chest was still there, but the pill had dulled it enough to push through. With a practiced hand, he raked his fingers through his hair and rolled his shoulders, willing himself to appear collected.

By the time he stepped back into the warm chaos of the pub, the cracks in his façade were hidden once more. Anthony called out a joke from the table, and Isaac smiled, raising his glass to join in the laughter. But as Penelope's radiant face came into view across the room, his grip on the glass tightened, and the numbness only seemed to hollow him further.

PART TWO

9

Hackney, London. 1997.

T he dull roar of the crowd echoed through the thin walls, a steady pulse of excitement that clashed violently with Isaac's spiraling thoughts. He sat on the cold, grimy floor of the dingy bathroom at the back of the venue, the overhead light flickering weakly, casting uneven shadows across the cracked tiles. His tight leather outfit—Anthony's idea, of course—clung uncomfortably to his skin, every inch of it making him itch.

Isaac's hands trembled as he worked the thin paper, rolling with precision born of desperation. He stared at the white line on the toilet seat, the faint gleam mocking him as his thoughts screamed louder than the crowd. His heart pounded as he lowered his head, inhaling sharply. The burn hit him instantly, searing up his nostrils and setting his nerves alight.

He winced, leaning his head back against the wall, the grime pressing against his damp hair. His ears buzzed, the cheers outside fading to a dull hum as the high crept in. The sharp edges of reality dulled, leaving behind a floating, hollow numbness.

Then, with a loud bang, the bathroom door slammed open, jolting Isaac slightly but not enough to break his haze. Heavy footsteps followed, the echo ringing out in the otherwise silent space.

"Isaac!" Anthony's voice was sharp, cutting through the fog.

Isaac blinked lazily, his head rolling to the side to see Anthony standing in the doorway of the stall, his expression a mix of fury and desperation. He said something else, but Isaac couldn't make out the words over the buzzing in his skull.

"Isaac!" Anthony barked again, stepping closer.

Isaac barely reacted, his mind detached, his body limp. Anthony cursed under his breath before lunging forward, grabbing Isaac by the collar of his shirt and hauling him to his feet with a force that sent the thin stall door clattering against its hinges.

"What the hell is wrong with you?!" Anthony shouted, shaking him violently. His words were muffled, barely penetrating Isaac's haze.

Isaac swayed, his knees threatening to buckle as his head lolled forward. He could see Anthony's mouth moving, his eyes wide with anger and fear, but it all felt distant, unreal.

Then came the punch.

Anthony's fist connected with Isaac's cheek in a solid, searing blow, snapping his head to the side and sending him stumbling against the stall. The sharp pain cut through the fog like a knife, bringing the high crashing down with brutal clarity.

Isaac groaned, his hand flying to his face as he glared at Anthony through blurry eyes. "What the hell, man?" he muttered, his voice slurred but audible now.

Anthony's nostrils flared, his fury unrelenting. "What the hell is wrong with you, Isaac? You're supposed to be on stage right now! You're screwing all of us over!"

Isaac shoved Anthony away, staggering toward the door with a scowl. "Get the fuck off me," he mumbled, ignoring the string of profanities that Anthony hurled at his back.

The hallway outside was dim and narrow, the thrum of the crowd growing louder as Isaac pushed through the backstage area. He emerged into the side stage, where the rest of the band was playing. Malcolm was at the drums, his arms moving in a blur as he kept a relentless rhythm. A few others, temporary fill-ins, rounded out the sound.

One of the guitarists caught sight of Isaac and grinned, giving him a quick wave before hurrying off stage to hand over his instrument. "Nice look," he joked, gesturing to the blood trickling from Isaac's nose.

Isaac smirked, wiping at his face with the back of his hand. "Thanks. Adds to the aesthetic."

Anthony stormed past him, his fury palpable as he grabbed the mic stand and bounded out onto the stage. The crowd erupted in cheers as his voice boomed over the speakers, his energy igniting the room despite the tension behind the scenes.

Isaac slung the guitar strap over his shoulder, testing the strings with a quick, practiced flick of his fingers. As he stepped beyond the curtain, the audience's screams grew deafening, the lights blinding him as they illuminated the stage in a harsh glare.

He couldn't see beyond the first row, the sea of faces lost to the brightness, but the sound was enough. It filled him, numbing the pain that lingered beneath his skin. His fingers moved instinctively, strumming out the familiar chords, the vibrations coursing through him.

Glancing back, he caught Malcom's glare, the expression hard as he maintained the pace. Isaac swallowed hard, pushing the guilt down deep as they built toward Anthony's solo.

The music carried him, but the weight in his chest never truly lifted.

The crowd surged with energy as Anthony leaned into the mic, belting out the lyrics with raw, unfiltered passion. His voice echoed through the venue, electrifying the room and sending waves of excitement through the audience. Isaac forced himself to stay focused, fingers moving across the strings with precision, but the tension between him and Anthony was palpable even from the stage.

Malcom pounded the drums harder, his jaw clenched as his eyes darted between Isaac and Anthony, silently willing the set to go off without any more issues. Isaac avoided eye contact, keeping his head down as the music reached its crescendo. The crowd's cheers were deafening, but they felt distant, like static in Isaac's ears.

As Anthony launched into his solo, Isaac stepped back toward the shadows of the stage, giving the spotlight to the frontman. Sweat dripped down his face, mixing with the blood still trickling from his nose. His hands trembled slightly as he gripped the guitar tighter, the high from earlier still lingering in the edges of his mind, keeping him just on the edge of control.

The song ended with a dramatic flourish, Anthony holding the final note as the crowd erupted into wild applause. Isaac followed the others offstage, his head pounding as they made their way to the cramped green room. The air was thick with the smell of sweat and beer, and the tension between him and Anthony hung like a storm cloud.

The moment the door shut, Anthony spun on him, shoving Isaac back against the wall.

"What the hell was that, Isaac?" Anthony snarled, his voice low but dangerous. "You're high out of your mind, and you think it's okay to just stroll on stage like nothing happened?"

Isaac shoved him back, his own anger flaring. "I handled it, didn't I? You're the one making a scene."

"You call that 'handling it'?" Anthony shot back, his voice rising. "You're falling apart, and you're dragging us down with you. This band isn't just about you, Isaac!"

Malcom stepped between them, his hands raised. "We don't need to do this here."

Anthony glared at Isaac for another long moment before backing off, running a hand through his sweat soaked hair. "Fine," he muttered, grabbing a bottle of water from the table and chugging it. "But this isn't over. You need to get your act together, or I'm done."

Isaac snorted, his lips curling into a bitter smile. "Sure. Like you'd walk away from all this. This is what you wanted, remember? This is all on you."

Anthony didn't respond, slamming the bottle down on the table before storming out of the room. "You're right. It is on me...consider yourself lucky tonight, Isaac. One more slip up and you're gone."

Isaac stormed out of the green room, leaving Anthony to brood in the corner. Exiting out the side door to stand in the alleyway behind the venue. It was dark, the air was warm but a contrast against his blistering hot skin. Malcom emerged to stand with him.

Malcom let out a long sigh, "You shouldn't test him, Isaac."

"I can't do this much longer Mal," Isaac started, his eyes misting with tears. Running a hand through his damp hair. "I can't pretend it's alright, when my existence is waging war on my mind."

"Your nightmares are worse?"

"Since Penelope left, I can't get rid of them...they rip me apart." Isaac glared at the hazy sky, daring the stars to show. "It's been two years. I should have gotten over her by now, moved on like I promised, but I can't stop how I feel about her."

"Has she called?"

Isaac shook his head, that was the hardest part, since Penelope left, there hadn't been one call, and when he attempted to contact her, he was refused. Anthony didn't talk about her, or tell Isaac how she was doing. It hurt to be shut out of her life completely.

"We've got one more set. Try to keep it together. I will try to talk to Anthony and get it all sorted."

Isaac didn't answer, just followed Malcom back inside, collapsing onto the worn-out couch in the corner of the room. The buzz from the earlier line had faded completely, leaving him feeling hollow and raw. He leaned his head back against the wall, closing his eyes as the sounds of the venue outside filtered in.

10

The golden morning light poured through the tall studio windows, streaking the polished wooden floor with warmth. The faint scent of rosin and sweat lingered in the air, mingling with the soft strains of the piano. Isaac stood in the doorway, his jacket hanging loosely over his shoulders, his hands buried deep in the pockets. His eyes scanned the room until they landed on Anthony, who was flipping through sheet music near the piano. The rhythmic scuffing of pointe shoes and hushed chatter from the dancers echoed softly, but Isaac barely noticed. His pulse thrummed loudly in his ears, his nerves taut as steel wires.

He stepped further inside, the slight creak of the floorboards betraying his presence. Anthony's head snapped up, his gaze locking on Isaac. His expression darkened instantly, a mix of frustration and concern flashing across his features.

"What're you doing here?" Anthony asked, his tone clipped but quiet enough not to draw attention.

Isaac hesitated, rubbing the back of his neck. "I came to talk."

Anthony set the music down with a sharp exhale, crossing his arms as he leaned against the piano. "About what? Last night? You mean the part where you were too high to come on stage. Or the part where you nearly got into a fight with me in the bathroom? Because, honestly, I'm not sure which pissed me off more."

Isaac flinched at the bluntness but nodded, his voice low. "Yeah, about that. I shouldn't have done it. I'm sorry, Anthony. I—" He faltered, his throat tightening. "I'm just... trying to cope, and it's not working. Not really."

Anthony's gaze softened slightly, but the tension in his posture remained. "Coping? You call that coping? Isaac, this isn't just about last night. It's about every time you've shown up late, barely sober, or completely strung out. You're a mess. And it's not just your problem—it's everyone's. You think I don't see why you're doing it to yourself?"

Isaac looked away, his jaw clenched. "I know I've been messing up. It's just... Penelope, she left, and—" His voice broke for a second, and he cleared his throat. "Ever since she's been gone, it feels like everything's caving in. I can't sleep. The nightmares are bad again. And when I wake up, it's like there's nothing left. Just... emptiness."

Anthony's shoulders dropped slightly, his own frustration giving way to concern. He stepped closer, lowering his voice. "I get it, Isaac. I really do. But drowning yourself in drugs isn't the answer. You're spiraling, and if you don't stop now, it's only going to get worse." He paused, his voice firm but not unkind. "Neil's already talking about rehab. If you keep this up, he's going to force your hand. Do you really want to go there?"

Isaac's head shot up, his eyes wide. "Rehab?"

Anthony nodded grimly. "Yeah, rehab. And honestly? Maybe it's what you need. But I'm telling you now, I don't want it to get to that point. I care about you. We all do. But you've got to start caring about yourself."

Isaac swallowed hard, his throat feeling dry as sandpaper. He nodded slowly, a knot tightening in his chest. "You're right," he admitted quietly. "I don't want to end up like this. I just... I don't know how to stop."

Before Anthony could respond, the click of heels echoed through the studio, and a tall woman with streaks of silver in her dark hair approached. She wore a sharp, tailored blazer over a flowing skirt, her posture commanding yet elegant. It was Madame Eloise, and she eyed the two men with a polite but curious smile.

"Anthony," she greeted with a nod before turning her attention to Isaac. "Mr. Maison, I haven't seen you here in ages. Are you here for the class?"

Isaac blinked, caught off guard. "Uh, no. I was just... talking to Anthony."

Madame Eloise tilted her head slightly, studying him. "Your expertise was always a breath of fresh air," she remarked. "Have you ever considered teaching? We could use someone with your energy and creativity in the studio. The students would love a fresh perspective."

Isaac froze, her words bouncing around in his mind. Teaching? The idea seemed absurd. He glanced at Anthony, who raised a brow, clearly waiting to see how Isaac would respond.

"I'll... think about it," Isaac finally said, his voice hesitant.

Madame Eloise smiled warmly. "Good. Let me know when you're ready. We could use you." She gave Anthony another nod before walking off, clapping her hands sharply to signal the start of the class.

Isaac exhaled deeply, running a hand through his messy hair. Anthony clapped him on the shoulder, his grip firm. "See? There's a way out of this. You've just gotta want it bad enough."

Isaac didn't respond, his gaze following the dancers as they began their warm-ups.

11

The familiar, dimly lit backstage of the theater buzzed with faint activity as Isaac made his way toward Neil's office. His footsteps echoed against the hardwood floors, each step slower than the last as unease coiled in his stomach. He'd been dodging Neil's calls for days, knowing his Uncle was wanting him to get back into his work at the theatre.

When Isaac entered, Neil was already seated behind his desk, a polished oak monstrosity buried under paperwork and a half-empty mug of coffee. His salt-and-pepper hair was neatly combed, but the worry lines etched deeply around his eyes told the story of someone who had been shouldering more than he let on. Neil gestured for Isaac to sit, his expression tight but softened by the hint of concern in his eyes.

"Isaac," Neil began, his tone flat but edged with disappointment. "We need to talk about your spending."

Isaac dropped into the chair, slouching back as he tried to avoid the direct gaze of his uncle. His hands fidgeted in his lap. "What about it?"

Neil leaned back in his chair, crossing his arms. "You're over-spending money, Isaac. Thousands have gone in the last month. The withdrawals are erratic—small sums, then big ones. You think I can't piece it together?"

Isaac's gaze fixed on the scuffed tips of his boots. "Yeah, I know what it looks like."

"It doesn't just look like it. I know it's drugs, Isaac," Neil's voice hardened, his usually calm demeanor nowhere to be found. "You've got a problem, and you need to get it under control. So here's how this is going to go: I've put a cut on your account. You'll get just enough for essentials—rent, food, travel—but no more surprises. And if I hear one more whisper about this nonsense, you're going to rehab."

Isaac nodded, his throat tight. "I get it, Neil."

"Time will tell, Isaac," Neil said, his tone softening just a fraction. "You know I wouldn't be doing this if I didn't care about you. You're family, Isaac. And I can't sit by and watch you destroy yourself like this."

Isaac swallowed hard, his eyes stinging as he nodded again.

Neil let the silence linger for a moment before shuffling some papers and moving to another topic. "Now, there's something else. The summer acting programs wrapped up, and we've got a few promising young talents. One of them is understudying for Two Gentlemen of Verona, but he needs experience shadowing a professional. That's where you come in."

Isaac raised a brow. "You want me to babysit?"

Neil shot him a warning look. "I want you to *mentor*. His name's Thomas Hidestone—he's bright, driven, and eager to learn. It's just a couple of weeks. He'll shadow you during workshops and rehearsals. Teach him the ropes, Isaac. It'll be good for both of you."

Isaac sighed, his shoulders sagging a little. "Fine. I'll meet him."

Neil smiled faintly, tapping his desk. "Good. He's in Studio B. Go introduce yourself."

Studio B was a smaller rehearsal space tucked away near the theater's back halls. The faint sounds of someone practicing lines filtered through the door. When Isaac stepped inside, he immediately spotted Thomas: a wiry teenager with a mop of curly ginger hair, pale skin, and eyes so bright blue they were almost startling. He was pacing the room, script in hand, muttering lines with exaggerated expressions, his movements full of nervous energy.

"Thomas?" Isaac said, his voice louder than necessary to break the boy's concentration.

The kid froze mid-pace, then turned quickly, his face lighting up with a bright smile. "That's me! And you're Isaac, right? Neil said you'd be coming by."

Isaac smirked, leaning against the doorframe. "Yeah, that's me. Guess I'm your mentor now."

Thomas bounded over, his energy infectious. "This is so cool! I've been reading all about your work, your performances. You're incredible. I mean, that monologue from Hamlet—chef's kiss!" He mimed the gesture, grinning. "I can't believe I get to learn from you."

Isaac chuckled, his amusement clear in his eyes as he watched the young actor's boundless enthusiasm. "You've got energy, I'll give you that," he said, his voice friendly and teasing. "So, understudy for Verona, huh? Which role?"

"Valentine," Thomas said proudly, clutching his script tightly to his chest. "It's been amazing so far, but I know I've got a lot to improve on. I'm ready to work hard, though. Whatever you've got to teach me, I'll soak it up like a sponge."

Isaac tilted his head slightly, a smirk tugging at his lips as he looked Thomas over. "A sponge, huh? We'll see how much you can absorb," he said, his tone playful as he crossed his arms. His eyes narrowed just a bit, and there was a teasing glint in them. "You got any plans after the workshop tonight?"

Thomas blinked, clearly caught off guard by the question. "Uh, no? Why?"

Isaac shrugged casually, his voice breezy. "My band's got practice later. Thought you might want to tag along. Get a sense of how stage presence works in different settings."

Thomas's eyes widened, his grin lighting up his face. "Are you serious? That would be amazing! Thank you!" he exclaimed, his excitement palpable.

Isaac couldn't help but chuckle at the kid's enthusiasm. "Alright then. Now, show me what you have so far," he said, his tone genuine as he stepped back, giving Thomas space to process.

Thomas nodded eagerly, clutching his script even tighter. "You got it!" he said, his voice full of determination.

Isaac watched him go back to his lines. Isaac found himself drawn to that innocence—so eager to please and soak up every bit of knowledge, completely missing the playful undertones of their conversation.

As they left the theater, Isaac led the way through the bustling streets of the city, the neon lights reflecting off the damp pavement from an earlier rain shower. Thomas followed, his chatter never missing a beat, his enthusiasm filling the air with a lively energy that seemed to chase away the shadows in Isaac's thoughts.

"—and then, at the summer camp, we did this play about, like, an enchanted forest! It was so cool! I was the fairy king, and I had to wear this giant crown made of leaves. It was kinda itchy, but totally worth it!" Thomas's voice was full of excitement, his hands animated as he spoke, gesturing wildly with his script.

Isaac nodded along, his eyes flicking between Thomas and the busy streets. The brightness in the younger man's eyes was distracting, but in a good way—it made it easier for Isaac to forget, just for a moment, about everything else going on in his life. "Sounds like you really enjoy acting," Isaac said, genuinely interested.

"Of course!" Thomas said, his grin widening. "I mean, it's my biggest passion! I can't imagine doing anything else. I'm saving up to go to RADA next year."

Isaac glanced over at him, impressed by the fire in Thomas's eyes. "RADA? That's ambitious. Got any backup plans if that doesn't work out?"

Thomas shrugged, his smile never faltering. "I'll figure it out when I get there. But honestly, it's all I've ever wanted. I can't imagine doing anything else but acting."

As they arrived at the rehearsal space, a small, nondescript building tucked away in a forgotten corner of the city, Isaac pushed open the door and held it for Thomas. The sound of loud music greeted them, a deep, rhythmic beat that vibrated through the walls. Inside, Anthony and Malcom were already setting up their equipment, positioning microphones and guitars on stage.

"Hey, look who's here," Anthony called out, looking up from the drumsticks he was arranging. "Who's this?"

Malcom leaned against the wall, his eyes crinkling with amusement. "Never thought I'd see the day," he said, smirking. "Isaac is a mentor."

Isaac rolled his eyes but smiled, motioning for Thomas to come inside. "Meet Anthony and Malcom," he said, his tone light and easy. "This is Thomas, he's the understudy for Valentine."

Thomas stepped forward, extending his hand with a wide grin. "I'm honored to meet you."

Anthony took his hand and gave it a firm shake. "Thomas, huh? Weren't you in the production last summer? Mustardseed, right?"

"Yeah, that's me," Thomas said, falling into awe as Isaac bent low to take out his guitar from the case near the window. "Wait...you're kidding me. You're *The Jacked Pistols*?" Seeing them all together seemed to click in the young man's expression.

Isaac grinned, clearly enjoying the moment. "Glad to know we have an honest fanbase."

Thomas's cheeks flushed as he shook his head fervently. "I've been listening to you guys for the past year. Your guitar riffs are insane. Honestly I would have loved to come to one of your shows if it wasn't for the late rehearsal nights at the theatre."

Malcom's gaze lingered on Thomas for a moment. "How old are you? Fifteen? Sixteen?"

Thomas puffed out his chest. "I'm seventeen, nearly eighteen."

Malcom snorted, flipping one of his drum sticks in hand, looking directly at Isaac. "Right. Well, don't let him near the beer fridge, then."

Thomas, blissfully unaware of the tension in Malcom's words, beamed as he stepped inside. "This is so cool. Thanks again for bringing me."

Isaac couldn't help but smile. "Don't mention it," he strummed the guitar, filling the place with a loud vibrating sound. "Now, let's get this rehearsal started."

The rehearsal space buzzed with energy as the band dove into another riff, the sound of Isaac's guitar slicing through the air like a blade. Isaac leaned into his instrument, letting the music flow through him, but his gaze drifted now and then to Thomas, perched on a beat-up old couch at the edge of the room. The kid was watching everything—every strum, every tap of the drums, every movement—with an intensity that rivaled Isaac's own when he was just starting out.

What caught Isaac's eye, though, was the way Thomas's fingers tapped rhythmically against his knee, almost unconsciously mirroring the beat of the song. It was subtle, but it showed an innate sense of timing that made Isaac's lips twitch into a grin.

As the song ended and the room settled into a hum of low chatter, Isaac pulled the strap of his guitar over his head, setting the instrument against its stand. Malcom got up to stretch his legs, Anthony wandered off to talk to the sound guys in the booth, and Isaac leaned against the wall, running a hand through his sweat-dampened hair.

Before he could reach for his own water bottle, Thomas was suddenly in front of him, holding one out with a shy smile. "Thought you might need this," Thomas said, his cheeks slightly pink from the attention.

Isaac raised an eyebrow but accepted the bottle, cracking it open. "Cheers, mate. You keep this up, and I'll start expecting room service after every set."

Thomas laughed nervously, rubbing the back of his neck. "I just thought... well, you've been playing nonstop. Looked like you could use it."

Isaac took a long drink, his eyes never leaving Thomas. There was something unguarded about him, something refreshing. He smirked, wiping his mouth with the back of his hand. "Tell you what, since you're so keen to help out, why don't you give it a go?"

Thomas blinked, confused. "Give what a go?"

Isaac nodded toward his guitar, still gleaming under the dim lights. "Playing. Come on, don't act like I didn't notice you tapping along like a pro over there. You've got rhythm."

Thomas's eyes widened, his hands going up in protest. "Oh no, I couldn't. I mean, not in front of you guys. You're all amazing. I'd embarrass myself."

Isaac leaned forward, his smirk softening into something more encouraging. "Don't sell yourself short, Thomas. No one's judging you here. Just pick it up and see what happens. Think of it as an improv class."

Thomas hesitated, glancing at the guitar like it might bite him. But Isaac didn't move, holding his ground until Thomas sighed and reached for it. "Alright, but don't laugh, okay?"

Isaac stepped back, crossing his arms as he watched Thomas settle the strap over his shoulder. It looked comically oversized on him at first, but as soon as Thomas's fingers touched the strings, all awkwardness disappeared.

The first few chords were cautious, tentative, but within moments, Thomas's confidence grew. His fingers moved over the frets with surprising precision, picking out a melody Isaac recognized immediately. It was one of the band's own songs, played with only a few minor mistakes.

Isaac's eyebrows shot up, impressed. "How long have you been playing?"

Thomas grinned sheepishly, his cheeks flushing again. "I've dabbled a bit, but nothing serious. I just really like your music, so I learned some of the riffs... for fun."

Isaac laughed, the sound warm and genuine. "*For fun*, he says. You've got some bloody talent. Don't let anyone tell you otherwise."

Thomas handed the guitar back, clearly relieved to be finished but glowing with pride. "You really think so?"

Isaac slung the guitar over his shoulder again, nodding. "I know so. Stick with it, and you'll be stealing my gigs before long."

Thomas chuckled, his nervousness fading. "Not a chance. You're way too good for that."

Isaac smirked, leaning in just enough to make Thomas's eyes widen slightly. "Flattery will get you everywhere, you know."

Before Thomas could respond, Malcom's voice cut through the moment. "Isaac! You planning on joining us, or are you running a music school now, too?"

Isaac rolled his eyes, straightening up. "Yeah, yeah." He glanced at Thomas one last time, the corners of his mouth quirking up. "You've got the goods, Thomas. Don't forget it."

PART THREE

12

Brixton, London. 1998.

T he dim hum of the pub surrounded Isaac like a cocoon, the bass from the music reverberating through his chest. The after party was in full swing, the air thick with laughter, clinking glasses, and the occasional burst of shouted conversation. Thomas was stationed near the door, manning a small booth piled high with merchandise. His grin was unwavering as he handed over a t-shirt to an excited fan, his enthusiasm contagious even from a distance.

Isaac leaned back in his seat, nursing a pint, but the creeping tendrils of unease began to crawl under his skin. Across from him, two girls were chatting animatedly, their voices lilting with flirtation as they edged closer to him. Normally, he'd enjoy the attention, play along, maybe even take things further. But tonight, their voices blended into the haze of the room, their words indistinct against the pounding of his pulse.

"I'll be back in a minute," he muttered, flashing a half-hearted smile as he pushed up from the booth. The girls barely acknowledged him, already lost in their own conversation.

The bathroom was dingy, lit by a flickering fluorescent bulb that cast harsh shadows on the cracked concrete walls. It smelled faintly of damp and old beer, the floor slick in places Isaac didn't care to inspect too closely. He let the door swing shut behind him, leaning against the cold wall as he tugged off his boot.

From its depths, he pulled out a small baggie, the pills inside rattling faintly. His hands trembled as he tipped them into his palm, his breath shallow and quick. Without hesitation, he tossed them back, swallowing hard and grimacing at the bitterness that lingered in his throat.

He moved to the sink, turning the rusty tap to let cold water gush over his hands. He splashed his face, the icy shock grounding him momentarily. He stared at his reflection in the cracked mirror, the dim light catching the sharp angles of his cheekbones, his slightly bloodshot eyes.

With a deep breath, Isaac left the bathroom, stepping back into the throbbing pulse of the pub. The pills were already beginning to work, a dulling haze settling over his nerves like a weighted blanket. He made his way to the bar, ordering another drink to chase the remnants of anxiety clinging to his chest.

Out of the corner of his eye, he spotted Anthony. He was standing near the edge of the bar, leaning in close to a man Isaac didn't recognize. The man's hand brushed against Anthony's, and jealousy flared hot and fast in Isaac's chest, burning through the fog. He clenched his jaw, gripping the edge of the bar so tightly his knuckles turned white.

Unable to sit still, Isaac pushed himself into the throng of people on the dance floor. The pills were in full effect now, his mind a pleasant blur as he lost himself in the music. A girl with dark curls and a sly smile slid up to him, pressing her body close as they moved together. Isaac smiled back, his charm automatic, but his eyes kept straying to the bar.

Anthony was watching him.

The realization sent a jolt through Isaac, the heat from the dance floor suddenly oppressive. "Sorry," he murmured to the girl, stepping back with a strained smile. She looked confused but shrugged, turning her attention to someone else as Isaac slipped away.

He found a dark hallway at the back of the pub, the noise of the crowd muffled here. Leaning against the wall, he tried to catch his breath, the weight of the evening pressing down on him.

"Isaac?"

The voice was soft but unmistakable. Isaac glanced up to see Anthony standing there, concern etched on his face.

"Are you alright?" Anthony asked, stepping closer.

Isaac opened his mouth to lie, to brush it off, but the words caught in his throat. The pills, the jealousy, the gnawing ache of something he couldn't name—it was all too much. "I'm fine," he said, his voice rough and unconvincing.

Anthony frowned, not buying it. "Hey, whatever it is, it'll get better," he said gently. "You've been through worse, haven't you?"

Isaac huffed a bitter laugh, his head tilting back against the wall. Anthony was so close now, his presence steadying in a way Isaac didn't want to think about too hard.

"You don't get it," Isaac whispered, his voice barely audible over the thrum of distant music. His eyes locked on Anthony's, his chest tight. "We shouldn't... This isn't..."

Anthony nodded slowly, his expression unreadable. "Yeah," he said, his voice just as soft. "We shouldn't."

But the space between them disappeared anyway. Their lips met in a kiss that was slow and tentative at first, then deeper, more desperate. Isaac's hands found Anthony's waist, pulling him closer as the world around them fell away. Desire coiled tighter in Isaac's chest as they clung together in the dark.

Sudden footsteps towards them broke the spell. Anthony pulled away and hurried back to the afterparty, leaving Isaac to hide in the corridor. Isaac was completely numb, his mind a blank shift as the pills took full effect, he staggered out to the front. Nodding to Malcom before he found Thomas.

"Isaac, we've just sold out," Thomas beamed, enthusiastically.

"That's great," Isaac winced, his mind already swimming. Sleep desperately wanted to come to him. "Would you help me home...bit off my tits."

"For sure," Thomas hastily grabbed his jacket. Waving to someone before stepping out into the cold beside Isaac.

The silence between them stretched taut for three blocks, each step weighed down by unspoken tension. They reached a corner where the streetlights cast their tired glow, and Isaac raised his hand to hail a cab. Thomas, unusually quiet, lingered beside him, his tall frame stiff with unease. His gaze flicked to Isaac, cautious and searching, while his fingers twitched at his sides as though he didn't know where to put them.

Inside the cab, the tension followed them like a third passenger. Thomas sat ramrod straight, stealing glances at Isaac, who pressed himself against the opposite door. The usually chatty Thomas remained silent, his wary eyes taking in Isaac's every fidget and the tremble in his hands. The ride passed in muted discomfort until they arrived near the flat Isaac shared with Malcom. As the cab pulled away, the street's stillness wrapped around them.

"Are you alright?" Thomas finally asked, his voice softer than usual, his large blue eyes brimming with concern.

"I'm fine," Isaac muttered, but his voice betrayed him, thin and strained. His skin burned under the cold night air, and his palms were slick with sweat as he fumbled in his pocket for his keys.

Thomas stepped closer, his hand reaching out when Isaac stumbled against the doorframe. "You don't look fine," he said, his tone firm but gentle.

Isaac hissed through clenched teeth, yanking his arm free. "I said I'm fine." He pushed the door open and staggered inside, leaving it ajar for Thomas, who followed without invitation.

The flat was suffocatingly quiet, the kind of silence that swallowed sound and left only the dull hum of your thoughts. The sharp contrast to the cacophony of the party they'd left behind made Isaac's head spin. His body still buzzed with the aftershocks of Anthony's kiss, his mind haunted by it, his anger simmering just below the surface. He turned abruptly, his glare sharp as a blade.

"You should leave," he snapped, pointing toward the door.

Thomas didn't budge. "I don't think I should."

Isaac scoffed, kicking off his boots with careless abandon. "Whatever. Just don't talk so much. It really hurts my brain," he muttered, staggering toward the kitchen.

"I could make tea," Thomas offered from the other room, his voice cautious. "Or order takeaway."

Isaac rolled his eyes, yanking open the fridge. "If you're hungry for that sort of thing," he muttered, grabbing a beer and cracking it open.

Thomas appeared in the doorway, his arms crossed. In the faint light of the kitchen, he looked taller, broader than when they'd first met. His wiry frame had filled out over the past year, but it wasn't just his stature that had changed. His blue eyes, once so bright with naivety, now held a weight that unnerved Isaac. They pinned him in place, unflinching and knowing.

"Should you be drinking?" Thomas asked, his tone steady.

Isaac slammed the can onto the counter and stepped closer, defiance radiating off him. Though Thomas was taller, Isaac closed the gap between them as if daring him to flinch. "I'm not drunk," he said, his voice low and sharp.

"I know," Thomas replied simply, unmoved.

Those eyes—damn them. They saw too much. This wasn't the same Thomas he'd met a year ago. That Thomas had been naive, almost annoyingly so, but this Thomas had grown into himself. He was sharp, steady, and unrelenting in a way Isaac found infuriating and unsettling.

"You're high," Thomas said, his voice cutting through the tension like a blade. There was no question, only certainty.

Isaac laughed bitterly, shaking his head. "Taking on Malcom's opinions now, are you?" he sneered, hoping sarcasm might deflect the conversation.

Thomas didn't flinch. "Mal didn't have to tell me. I've known a fair few addicts. My cousin spent a year in a private institution up north."

Isaac's jaw tightened. "I am not an addict. I have nightmares."

"So does my cousin," Thomas said, his tone flat. "From the war. We all carry things, Isaac. You're not special. There's no outrunning the weight."

"You don't understand," Isaac snapped, his voice trembling with anger and something more fragile.

"I don't have to understand to see that you're in pain," Thomas countered, his voice softening. "And I know I'm not the only one who doesn't want to see you like this."

"Is this supposed to be an intervention?" Isaac spat, narrowing his eyes.

Thomas reached into his pocket and pulled out an envelope. The insignia on the letterhead made Isaac's stomach twist. He recognized it instantly, the ache in his chest sharp and immediate. His throat tightened as he realized what it meant. Of course, they would send Thomas. Who else could hand him this without risking a fight? Anthony would have threatened him, Malcom would have reasoned with him, but Thomas... Thomas disarmed him in ways neither of them could.

"How long?" Isaac whispered, the words barely audible as tears pricked his eyes.

"Six months," Thomas said softly. "You'd be out by summer. It's a new year, Isaac. Start it right."

13

The smell of rosin and polished wood hit Isaac the moment he stepped into the ballet school, stirring memories that felt both distant and immediate. It had been six months—a lifetime, it seemed—since he'd been in this space. The familiar creak of the floor beneath his trainers, the faint strains of piano music filtering through the halls, and the echo of dancers' voices all felt like fragments of a world he was still trying to re-enter.

Isaac shifted the strap of his duffle bag on his shoulder, nerves tightening in his chest. His rehab was behind him, but the thought of seeing Anthony again, of facing the man he'd been running from even before everything fell apart, made him hesitate at the door. He exhaled sharply, steeling himself, and walked inside.

The main studio was busy, the sound of feet striking the floor in perfect rhythm punctuated by the instructor's clipped commands. Isaac lingered in the doorway, scanning the room for Anthony. He wasn't there. Disappointment, sharp and bitter, flickered through him, but Isaac swallowed it down.

He set his bag against the wall and stripped off his hoodie, revealing a leaner frame than before, his muscles softer from months of disuse. Joining the class, Isaac fell into the familiar routine of pliés and tendus, his movements tentative at first. His legs felt stiff, his balance unsteady, but as he pushed through the exercises, muscle memory began to kick in. The rhythm of the class, the focus on each movement, helped dull the edge of his nerves.

After the class ended, Isaac wiped the sweat from his brow with the hem of his shirt and stretched out his legs, the ache in his muscles already settling in. He reached for his water bottle when he spotted someone down the hall—a familiar figure, her long, dark hair tied in a sleek bun, her frame poised and graceful even at rest.

"Penelope?" he called, his voice echoing faintly in the empty corridor.

She turned at the sound of his voice, her expression sharp with surprise before it shifted into something cooler. She didn't move to meet him, instead staying rooted where she stood.

"Isaac," she said, her tone clipped.

He walked toward her, a hesitant smile tugging at his lips. "What are you doing here? I thought you were in New York."

Her arms folded over her chest, and she tilted her chin slightly, a defensive posture that wasn't lost on him. "Plans change," she replied curtly. "I'm surprised to see you here, dancing."

The words stung more than he cared to admit, but Isaac forced his smile to remain. "Yeah, well... trying to get back into it, you know? Thought I'd ease my way in."

Penelope's gaze flicked over him, assessing, but her expression gave nothing away. "Good for you." Her words were polite, but there was no warmth behind them.

Isaac shifted uncomfortably under her scrutiny. "Have you come back to dance?"

"No," she cut in, her voice firm. "I just came to collect the remainder of my collection from madame, she had them saved for me."

The bluntness of her words hit him like a blow to the chest. Isaac opened his mouth to respond, but Penelope was already turning away. "Take care of yourself, Isaac," she said over her shoulder before disappearing around the corner, leaving him standing there, alone in the hallway.

The silence that followed was deafening. Isaac ran a hand through his damp hair, frustration bubbling under the surface. He wasn't sure what he had expected from Penelope, but her coldness left him shaken.

He picked up his bag and slung it over his shoulder, the weight of it pressing into him as he walked back toward the door. The school no longer felt as welcoming as it had when he first stepped inside. The ghosts of his past, of what he had done, of who he had hurt, lingered in every corner.

14

The theatre hummed with quiet activity as actors rehearsed lines, stagehands adjusted set pieces, and the faint sound of the orchestra tuning their instruments drifted from the pit. Isaac stood just off-stage, leaning against a wall, his hands shoved deep into his jacket pockets as he watched Anthony direct the blocking of the next scene.

Anthony had an air of quiet authority, his movements sharp and deliberate as he gestured toward the actors and corrected their positions. His voice, though calm, carried easily over the murmur of the stage crew. Isaac couldn't help but admire him, even as the weight of unanswered questions pressed against his chest.

When there was a pause in the rehearsal, Isaac seized the opportunity. He approached Anthony, his boots echoing softly on the wooden stage floor.

"Hey," Isaac began, trying to keep his voice casual. "Can I have a word?"

Anthony glanced at him, his expression unreadable, before nodding. "Make it quick. We've got a lot to get through."

They moved to the side of the stage, away from the activity, where the shadows of the wings offered a small measure of privacy. Isaac hesitated, running a hand through his hair before speaking.

"I saw Penelope at the school yesterday," he said. "She's back."

Anthony's jaw tightened, but he said nothing, his eyes fixed on a distant point over Isaac's shoulder.

Isaac frowned at his silence. "What's going on with her? She's supposed to be in New York. Did she find out about...me?" His voice dropped at the last word, the implication of his time in rehab hanging heavily between them.

Anthony's gaze snapped back to Isaac, his expression hard. "No, she doesn't know. And this has nothing to do with you or rehab."

"Then what is it?" Isaac pressed. "I know something's wrong. Just tell me."

Anthony sighed, dragging a hand over his face. "It's not my place—"

"Is it because of us?" Isaac interrupted, his voice low but urgent. "Because of the kiss? I—look, I'm sorry. I didn't mean to make you break your vows. I shouldn't have—"

Anthony cut him off with a sharp laugh, one that was equal parts amusement and exasperation. "Isaac, stop. That kiss? It's not what's keeping me up at night."

Isaac blinked, taken aback. "You're not worried about it?"

Anthony shook his head, a small, wry smile tugging at his lips. "I'm not. And just to prove it..." He leaned in, his hand brushing lightly against Isaac's arm before his lips met Isaac's in a brief, deliberate kiss. It was soft but resolute, filled with an assurance that left Isaac momentarily breathless.

When Anthony pulled back, his gaze was steady. "See? No guilt. But, Isaac…" His tone shifted, becoming firm. "We're not going down that road again. Whatever happened between us—it can't happen again."

Isaac swallowed hard, his chest tight. "I get it. I do. But you have to tell me what's going on with Penelope. I'm worried, Anthony. She didn't look right, and the way she spoke to me, there's something you're not saying."

Anthony hesitated, the mask of his composure slipping just enough for Isaac to see the tension beneath. Finally, he exhaled heavily, leaning back against the wall.

"She's home because she had to drop out of her contract," Anthony said quietly. "She's… she has cancer."

Isaac's breath caught, the word hitting him like a punch to the gut. "Cancer?" he echoed, his voice barely above a whisper. "Is she—?"

"She's recovering from surgery," Anthony cut in, his tone steady but tinged with weariness. "They caught it early, they think, but she's going to need treatment. Chemo, radiation—whatever the doctors decide after her scans."

Isaac stared at him, the weight of the revelation settling heavily on his shoulders. "God, Anthony… I didn't know. I—"

Anthony placed a hand on Isaac's shoulder, grounding him. "She didn't want people to know, Isaac. She's been keeping it quiet, focusing on getting better. She's strong—she'll get through this."

Isaac nodded, though the lump in his throat made it hard to speak. "I just… I wish I'd known sooner. Maybe I could've…"

"There's nothing you could've done," Anthony said gently but firmly. "Just… be there for her. When she's ready."

Isaac nodded again, his heart heavy with guilt and concern. The theatre around them felt distant, the noise of the rehearsal a dull hum in the background. For the first time in months, Isaac felt truly sober, the clarity cutting through him like a blade.

15

The darkness clung to Isaac like a second skin, heavy and suffocating as he jolted awake, his chest heaving with ragged breaths. The nightmare had been vivid—too vivid. His heart pounded, the echoes of fear still coursing through his veins. Sweat slicked his skin, soaking the collar of his shirt. Isaac sat up, gripping the edge of the mattress as if it might steady the maelstrom in his mind.

The pull of the pills was there, a shadowy whisper in the back of his thoughts. It would be so easy, the craving murmured. Just one, and the pain would dull, the world would quiet. But Isaac shook his head violently, forcing the thought away. He wasn't going back down that road. Not again.

Instead, he threw on a hoodie and running shoes, the cold night air biting against his flushed skin as he stepped out into the street. The city was quiet, bathed in the muted glow of streetlights and the occasional flicker of a passing car. Isaac took off at a jog, his feet pounding against the pavement in a rhythmic escape. His breathing was uneven at first, but soon it steadied, matching the cadence of his steps. He pushed himself harder, running through the stillness as though he could out-run the memories clawing at him.

By the time he returned to his flat, his muscles were aching, and his lungs burned in a way that was almost comforting. The faint sound of someone calling his name made him pause as he approached the building.

"Isaac, dear! Have you seen Morris?"

It was Mrs. Jennings, his elderly neighbor from two doors down. She stood on the sidewalk in a wool coat that looked too big for her, her frail hands clutching a torch. Her small frame seemed lost in the dim light, her eyes wide with worry.

Isaac jogged over, his breath still coming in shallow bursts. "Morris gone missing again?" he asked, though he already knew the answer.

"Yes," she said, her voice trembling slightly. "He slipped out while I was putting the bins out. I've been looking for him everywhere."

Isaac gave her a reassuring smile. "Don't worry, Mrs. Jennings. I'll find him."

He started combing the nearby streets and alleys, looking out for the stubborn tabby. After a few minutes, a soft rustling caught his attention from a hedgerow near the parking lot. Isaac crouched down, peering into the shadows. "Morris? That you, buddy?"

A pair of glowing green eyes blinked back at him, and a second later, the cat slinked out with an indignant meow. Isaac scooped him up, stroking the soft fur as Morris half heartedly squirmed, but finally settled under his arm.

"Got him!" Isaac called as he returned to Mrs. Jennings, who sighed in visible relief.

"Oh, thank heavens," she said, taking Morris into her arms. "You're a saint, Isaac."

"It's no trouble," he said, grinning. "Anything else I can do?"

"Well, since you're offering," she said hesitantly, "I do have an order waiting at the shop, but my hip's been acting up something terrible. If you're heading that way..."

"I'll grab it for you," Isaac interrupted, already walking toward the door. "Consider it done."

The corner shop was quiet, save for the low hum of fluorescent lights. Isaac picked up Mrs. Jennings's bag, a modest haul of groceries and started toward the exit when he spotted Penelope by the produce section. She was dressed in a thick jacket, her hair pulled into a low bun. She looked like she didn't want to be seen, her eyes scanning the shelves with sharp focus.

"Penelope," Isaac called, his voice tentative.

She turned slowly, her expression cool, the same detached indifference she'd shown him at the ballet school. "Isaac," she said flatly, giving him a once over. "Didn't expect to see you here."

"Just running an errand for Mrs. Jennings," he said, holding up the bag. "What about you? Stocking up on oranges?"

"Something like that," she said, tucking a strand of hair behind her ear.

Isaac shifted awkwardly, unsure how to bridge the gap between them. "Look, I don't know why you've been avoiding me, but—"

"I haven't been avoiding you," she cut in, though the defensive edge in her voice said otherwise. "I've been busy."

"Of Course," Isaac said, trying to keep his tone light. "Too busy to come to band practice?"

That earned a small, almost imperceptible twitch of her lips. "Band practice, huh?"

"Yeah. You should come by. We're rehearsing tomorrow night."

Penelope hesitated, her gaze flickering briefly to the floor. "I'll think about it," she said finally, her voice softer.

"I'd like that," Isaac said sincerely. "I mean, we'd all like that."

She nodded, then turned back to the shelf, effectively ending the conversation. Isaac watched her for a moment longer, wondering what weight she was carrying and why she wouldn't let him help. Finally, he turned and left, heading back to Mrs. Jennings's flat to drop off her groceries.

The rehearsal space was alive with energy, Anthony and Malcom were tuning their guitars while Thomas arranged cables near the amplifiers, chattering about a new riff he wanted to try. Isaac strummed absentmindedly, lost in his own thoughts, when the sound of the door opening drew everyone's attention.

Penelope stepped inside, dressed simply in jeans and a loose sweater. Her ballet posture still gave her an air of effortless grace, but her face was pale, and her eyes held a guarded expression. The room quieted for a moment, the others exchanging quick glances before Anthony broke the silence.

"Hey, Nel," he said casually, his voice kind but reserved.

She gave a faint smile. "Hey. I figured I'd stop by and see if you all still know how to play." Her attempt at levity didn't quite land, but no one pushed her on it.

Isaac stood, his heart thudding. "Penelope. Glad you came."

She nodded, avoiding his gaze as she moved toward an empty chair by the wall. "Don't mind me. Just pretend I'm not here."

The band resumed, launching into a familiar song. Isaac tried to focus, but his attention kept drifting to Penelope. She sat stiffly, her arms crossed, her eyes fixed on the floor. After they wrapped up a set, Isaac grabbed a bottle of water and approached her.

"Can we talk?" he asked softly, glancing back at the others. Anthony was studiously avoiding looking at them.

Penelope's expression tightened. "What about?"

"Not here," Isaac said. "Just...outside?"

She hesitated before sighing and standing. They stepped out into the alley behind the studio, the chill of the evening air wrapping around them. Isaac stuffed his hands into his jacket pockets, unsure how to start.

"I know about the cancer," he said finally, his voice low.

Penelope's head snapped up, her eyes narrowing. "Anthony told you?" she asked sharply.

"I...bullied it out of him," Isaac admitted, cringing. "I'm sorry. I just—"

"You had no right," she interrupted, her tone cutting. "It's my business, not yours."

"I know," he said quickly. "You're right. But I care about you, Penelope. And I want to be here for you. Whatever you need."

Her shoulders tensed, and for a moment, Isaac thought she might walk away. But then she let out a slow breath, her gaze softening just a fraction. "What are you going to do, Isaac? Sit in on my chemo sessions? Hold my hand during scans?"

"If that's what you want, then yeah," he said earnestly. "I'll do it. I'll bring snacks and bad jokes. Or I'll just sit quietly and let you yell at me if that helps."

A ghost of a smile tugged at her lips, but it quickly faded. "You don't owe me anything."

"This isn't about owing," Isaac said. "You've always been there for me, even when I didn't deserve it. Let me do the same for you."

Penelope studied him for a long moment, her expression unreadable. Finally, she nodded, though her voice was hesitant. "Fine. I have a scan on Thursday. You can meet me at the hospital."

Isaac's heart lightened. "Okay. What time?"

"Seven a.m.," she said, almost daring him to object.

He grinned faintly. "I'll be there. Don't be surprised if I show up with muffins."

She rolled her eyes but didn't argue, turning to head back inside. Isaac watched her go, his heart heavy yet hopeful. There was so much he couldn't fix, so much he couldn't take away, but for once, he felt like he might be able to help. And he wasn't going to let her face this alone.

16

The hospital was colder than Isaac had anticipated. Even with the sterile smell of disinfectant and the low hum of machines in the background, the place felt suffocating. He sat in the waiting area outside the radiology wing, his legs jittering as Penelope went in for her scans. She had waved him off with a small smile, insisting she'd be fine, but her pale face betrayed her nerves.

After what felt like hours, a nurse called her name again for blood draws, leaving Isaac alone. Restless, he stood and made his way toward the café down the hall, his boots echoing against the polished floors.

The café was small, tucked into a corner of the hospital with a counter offering overpriced coffee and pastries that looked days old. Isaac ordered a black coffee and leaned against the counter as he waited, his gaze drifting to the vending machines and the handful of patients milling about.

The sharp, clinical smell of the hospital mixed with the scent of burnt coffee triggered something deep in his mind. A flash of a memory hit him—a sterile room, the beep of a heart monitor, his own small body curled in a bed as doctors spoke in hushed tones to a social worker nearby. The echoes of his mothers's screams replayed in his head, loud and sudden.

Isaac's chest tightened, his breath catching. He abandoned the coffee on the counter, pushing through the café doors and down the hall, his legs moving on autopilot until he found an exit leading to the stairwell by the parking garage. The cool air of the unheated space hit his flushed skin as he dug into his jacket pocket for his cigarettes.

He lit one with shaking hands, his fingers barely able to hold the lighter steady. The first drag filled his lungs, but it did little to calm the chaos in his mind. He paced the small concrete landing, his breath visible in the chilly air.

The memory wouldn't leave him. His mother's terrified face as she hugged him. Running through the woods. Waking up in a hospital bed surrounded by doctors. Terrified and calling for his mum, but she never came. Isaac remembered the nights he dreamt of them. He clenched his jaw, forcing the images back, but his body wouldn't stop shaking.

"Isaac?"

The soft voice startled him, and he turned to see Penelope standing at the bottom of the stairs. She was bundled in her coat, her scarf loosely draped around her neck. Her expression softened when she saw the cigarette in his hand and the panic in his eyes.

"I'm sorry," he muttered, crushing the cigarette under his boot. "I just needed a minute."

She stepped closer, her boots crunching on the concrete. "What's wrong?"

Isaac rubbed a hand over his face, feeling the burn of shame in his chest. "I— It's stupid," he said, his voice strained. "This place... hospitals... I just— It gets to me."

Penelope tilted her head, her brows furrowing. "Why?"

He hesitated, the words catching in his throat. But then he looked at her, at the patience in her eyes, the quiet strength she carried even now and something cracked open inside him.

"When I was a kid," he began, his voice barely above a whisper, "I spent a lot of time in hospitals. After... after my family disappeared." He paused, swallowing hard. "They found me wandering Queens Woods alone, bloodied...they told me my father killed my mum... that he must have tried me too but I got away. I don't remember," Isaac shook his head. "All I remember was waking up in the hospital...poked and prodded. Institutionalized for nearly a year because of the night-mares."

Penelope's lips parted in astonishment, but she didn't interrupt. She stepped closer, her hand resting gently on the stair rail as she listened.

Isaac exhaled shakily, running a hand through his hair. "I was just a kid, you know? I didn't understand why it happened or why they put me in this place where everything smelled like antiseptic, and no one talked to me unless it was about paperwork or my bruises. It's stupid to still be scared of it, but... I can't help it."

Penelope's hand came up slowly, her fingers brushing his arm before settling there. "It's not stupid," she said softly. "It's trauma, Isaac. It stays with you, even when you think it's gone."

He nodded, his throat too tight to speak. She stepped closer, her warmth cutting through the cold air of the stairwell. Her expression was tender, filled with a quiet understanding that made his chest ache.

"I didn't know," she said after a moment, her voice barely above a whisper. "I'm so sorry."

"Not many know, except Malcom, and Anthony in part..." He shook his head. "Fuck, I'm sorry. You've got enough to deal with. I didn't mean to dump this on you."

Penelope reached up and pressed a soft kiss to his cheek, her lips warm against his cold skin. "You've been here for me. Let me be here for you, too."

Isaac closed his eyes, letting the moment settle around them. For the first time in a long while, he felt like he wasn't completely alone.

17

The late afternoon sunlight streamed through the large windows of Neil's townhouse, casting warm hues across the vintage furniture and shelves brimming with books. Isaac sat on the edge of the worn leather sofa, his knee bouncing as he waited for Neil to return with tea. He fiddled with the hem of his sleeve, rehearsing the words in his mind. He wasn't sure how his uncle would respond to what he was about to ask.

Neil entered the room with a tray, setting it down on the low coffee table. His movements were careful, deliberate, as they always were. He was a man of composed elegance, his years of traveling and living abroad reflected in his eclectic taste and refined demeanor.

"You're quiet today," Neil said, pouring tea into delicate porcelain cups. His sharp, gray eyes glanced up at Isaac as he handed him a cup. "Something on your mind?"

Isaac took the tea, but he didn't sip it. He kept his gaze on the steam curling from the cup, trying to gather his thoughts. "Yeah, there is," he said finally, his voice subdued. "I wanted to talk to you about someone. Someone important."

Neil raised an eyebrow, settling into the armchair across from Isaac. He rested his elbow on the armrest, his chin on his hand. "Important?" he echoed, a faint smile playing on his lips. "This sounds intriguing. Go on."

Isaac hesitated, feeling the weight of the moment. "Her name is Penelope. She's... someone I've known for a while. She's—" He stopped himself, unsure how much to share. "She's been through a lot recently. And I wanted to ask you something that involves her."

Neil's smile faded slightly, his expression turning more serious. "Go on," he said, leaning forward slightly.

"She's... she's ill," Isaac admitted, the words coming out heavier than he'd expected. "Cancer. She's recovering from surgery right now, but she's got treatments coming up. It's been hard for her. Really hard."

Neil's brows knit together, a flicker of concern in his eyes. "I'm sorry to hear that," he said quietly. "What is it you're asking, Isaac?"

Isaac set the cup down on the table, unable to sit still. He leaned forward, resting his elbows on his knees. "Her birthday's coming up, and I want to do something for her. Something special." He glanced at Neil, gauging his reaction before continuing. "I was thinking... maybe I could take her to Paris. Just for a little while. To get away, you know? To give her something to look forward to."

Neil's eyes narrowed slightly, but not with disapproval—more with thoughtfulness. "Paris?" he repeated. "And you'd like to use the apartment?"

Isaac nodded. "It's just sitting there, and I thought... maybe it could be a way for her to have some peace. A change of scenery. I think it could help her. Even if it's just for a week or two."

Neil leaned back in his chair, his gaze distant as he considered the request. The apartment in Paris was one of his favorite places—a sanctuary he rarely shared with anyone. But he also wasn't the type to deny Isaac something meaningful. After a long pause, he looked back at his nephew.

"You care about her," Neil said, more as a statement than a question.

Isaac nodded again, his voice steady. "I do. She's been there for me when I needed it. And I want to be there for her now."

Neil studied him for a moment, then sighed. "I'll admit, I'm hesitant. Not because I don't trust you, but because I don't know how she'll feel about this. A trip like that—it's intimate. Personal. Are you sure she'd be comfortable with it?"

Isaac shifted in his seat. "I'm not trying to pressure her. I'll talk to her about it first, obviously. I just... I want to give her something good."

Neil's expression softened, and he nodded slowly. "Alright," he said. "You have my permission. But promise me this, Isaac—if she says no, or if she's unsure, you won't push her. Let her decide."

"I promise," Isaac said quickly, relief washing over him. "Thank you, Uncle. Really."

Neil gave him a small smile. "You've got a good heart, Isaac. Just make sure she knows it's not about pity. People in her situation can be... sensitive to that."

"I will," Isaac assured him. "It's not about that. It's about... giving her a moment to feel alive again."

Neil nodded, his smile lingering. "Then I hope the city of light gives her exactly that."

The hospital room was filled with a quiet hum, the machines working steadily beside the bed, a bag filled with orange red pumping through the tubing into the catheter that disappeared under her half zipped hoodie. Penelope was nestled under a plush, pastel pink blanket, her half zip hoodie slightly askew over her frail shoulders. Her face, though pale, glowed softly in the muted light. Isaac sat a few feet away, his hands clasped loosely between his knees, his gaze wandering over the pictures adorning the walls.

The colorful drawings from Penelope's younger cousins were taped up alongside a collage of Polaroids, their corners curling with age. His eyes lingered on one particular Polaroid: Anthony and Isaac at fifteen, laughing in the golden light of a summer afternoon. Next to it, another photo of Penelope with her friends from ballet school—graceful, laughing, alive.

"You're drifting again," Penelope's soft voice broke through his thoughts.

He turned, catching her curious gaze over the edge of the book resting in her hands.

"I was looking at your pictures," Isaac said, nodding toward the wall. "I can't believe you still have that one."

Penelope followed his gaze, her thin fingers brushing against the peeling edge of the Polaroid of Anthony and Isaac. She smiled, a nostalgic warmth lighting her eyes.

"I'd just gotten my Polaroid camera for Christmas," she murmured. "Anthony saved up a week's worth of allowance—and, apparently, some extra chores—to buy it for me."

Isaac chuckled softly. "I remember that. I took him to four different shops to find the exact one."

Her eyes sparkled, glancing up at him. "You've always been so good," she said quietly.

His smile faltered. "That was a rough year. It was the first Christmas after I came back from France."

Penelope nodded, closing her book with a deliberate motion. "Your boarding school," she said knowingly. "Anthony told me your uncle pulled you out, but he didn't explain why."

Isaac shifted in his seat, his heart beating faster. He hesitated, rubbing the back of his neck. "He didn't know the real reason," he admitted. "I don't think I've ever had the heart to tell him."

Her brows knit together in concern, and she set her book aside, giving him her full attention. "What happened?"

Isaac exhaled, the words heavy as they formed. "One of my profes sors... she took advantage—" He paused, searching for the right words. "The dean found out. He told my uncle."

Penelope's eyes widened, and she instinctively reached for his hand, her touch gentle but firm. "That's awful, Isaac. Truly."

He nodded, his lips pressing into a thin line. "I haven't been back since, even though my mum's side of the family is still there."

"Not even once?" she asked, tilting her head.

"Well, my uncle still owns an apartment in Paris," Isaac said, his voice softening. Then, a spark lit his expression. "Have you ever been to Paris?"

Penelope's face softened as she shifted under her blanket, waving off his concern when she winced. "I went once, when I was six. Gran took me. I remember the Eiffel Tower and some carousel, but I haven't been since."

Isaac leaned forward, a nervous excitement brimming in his chest. "Would you like to go again?"

Her laugh was light but brief, her brow arching skeptically. "You're serious?"

"I am," he said, his voice firm and sincere. He reached out, taking her hand and brushing his lips against her fingers. "I want to take you to Paris, Penelope. I want to show you all my favorite places and eat the best croissants and éclairs. You'd love it."

Her smile returned, softer this time. "I'll go with you," she said, then added with a playful smirk, "but only if you spend Christmas with us."

Isaac leaned back, the rush of excitement dimming slightly. "Will that be alright? After, you know…"

She laughed, a light, tinkling sound that made his heart ache. "My father has forgiven you for swearing at Mass."

His cheeks reddened at the memory. "It was the first and last time I stepped into a church," he admitted, grinning sheepishly. "But in my defense, it wasn't entirely my fault."

"Oh, I know," Penelope teased, her eyes narrowing in amusement. "Anthony confessed his transgressions to me—well, most of them. Let's just say the slip of a hand during prayer is rather scandalous to imagine in such a setting."

Isaac groaned, covering his face with his hands as she laughed again. Despite everything, her laughter filled the room like sunlight breaking through clouds, and Isaac couldn't help but smile.

18

Snow blanketed the countryside, the stark white contrasting with the warm glow emanating from the windows of the Mooren household. Isaac adjusted his scarf as he stood on the doorstep, a twinge of nerves fluttering in his chest. The muffled hum of laughter and conversation reached his ears before the door opened to reveal Anthony, dressed in a forest-green sweater that made his blue eyes stand out even more.

"You made it," Anthony said, a welcoming grin spreading across his face as he stepped aside to let Isaac in.

Inside, the house was bustling with life. Penelope's younger cousins darted between the living room and the kitchen, squealing with excitement over their gifts. The scent of roasted meats, mulled cider, and fresh pine filled the air. Every corner of the room was adorned with Christmas decorations—garlands draped over the mantle, twinkling lights strung along the staircase, and a towering tree glittering with ornaments.

Penelope's and Anthony's parents were stationed in the kitchen, chatting lively. While Penelope sat near the fire, wrapped in a soft blanket, her face alight as she laughed at something her uncle was saying. The sight of her warmed Isaac's heart, even as it squeezed painfully in his chest. She looked more fragile than she had a year ago, but the fire in her eyes remained undimmed.

"Come on, everyone's been waiting," Anthony said, clapping Isaac on the shoulder. Isaac followed him through the room, meeting uncles, aunts, and cousins who all seemed genuinely delighted to meet "the man Penelope hasn't stopped talking about."

"There he is!"

"Hey Gran, you remember Isaac," Anthony smiled, as the warm embrace of the elderly woman with an equally warm embrace took Isaac in her arms.

"Of course I remember," Rhonda smiled. "It was a remarkable remembrance to see my darling Ray was up in arms at the young man that took the lord's name in vain. I remember a time when he himself swore at a cleric."

"I was only six, mama." Ray himself came into the room. Bringing with him a broad smile as he wrapped his arm around his mother.

Anthony flushed, giving Isaac a sideways glance. "Isaac wasn't raised in the church, Gran."

"A respectable boy," came the gruff voice of Rhonda's husband, Jon, in front of the couch, raising a glass of bubbling liquid. "Wasn't he the boy that brought flowers to Rhonda when she broke her foot."

Penelope smiled, taking her grandad's hand, glancing at Isaac. "Yes, he was granddad."

"How about Malcom," Anthony's mother, Angela, peered in through the kitchen.

"He had shifts at the clinic, he will spend Christmas with Neil."

Isaac smiled warmly, being pulled by the arm by Rhonda to sit in the living room next to her husband. Jon Mooren talked of current events, and those of the family that were still in the Netherlands. Isaac listened, the best he could, all the while Penelope kept her hand in his.

Jon chuckled, his deep voice resonating warmly. He leaned forward, peering at Isaac over the rim of his glass. "I've always been curious—where's your family from? I heard you spent some time in France, but Anthony said your grandfather is from Lebanon."

Isaac nodded, shifting slightly. "That's true, my grandfather is from Beirut. He moved to France when he was a young man."

Jon raised an eyebrow, intrigued. "Beirut? A beautiful city, I've heard, though troubled in its time."

Isaac's smile turned reflective, his gaze softening. "It is beautiful, and complicated. My grandfather used to tell me stories of the old souks and the Mediterranean Sea glimmering under the sun. He loved the energy of the city—the smells of spices, the sound of the call to prayer. He left in 1951, then he met my grandmother in France. It wasn't safe to stay, and he wanted a better life for his family."

Penelope, still holding Jon's hand, looked at Isaac with quiet admiration. "Did he ever talk about going back?"

"Always," Isaac said. "He used to say that no matter where you go, a part of your heart stays in the place you're from. But he made a life in France, and housed me every summer before I went to boarding school."

Rhonda leaned forward from her chair, her eyes bright. "Your grandfather sounds like a remarkable man. Did you get to know him well?"

Isaac nodded, his voice softening with affection. "He was a storyteller, always weaving tales of Beirut's golden days. When I was little, he taught me to cook Lebanese dishes—tabbouleh, kibbeh, things like that. He said it was important to keep our traditions alive, even if we were far from home. I was also taught the languages of both my grandparents. And the traditional dances."

Jon nodded approvingly, raising his glass again.

Anthony smirked, elbowing Isaac lightly. "Is that where you get your obsession with dance? He put one of Penelope's old partners to shame, and scolded him in the middle of class."

Isaac laughed, holding his hands up in surrender. "A mild correction."

Penelope's cheeks flushed, but she smiled, her grip tightening slightly. "Isaac's being modest. He has a natural gift for it. I convinced him to pick it back up, and he did. Isaac teaches classes there every week when he isn't at the theatre with his uncle."

"Marvelous," Rhonda was delighted.

"How about your uncle, these days?" Ray stood near them, joining into the conversation. Isaac felt his stomach begin to flop. "I haven't spoken to him since we put Anthony in primary. That was just after you went back to school."

"He's busy, he owns a production company as well as the theatre," Isaac felt tight.

"It's a mighty shame," Ray continued, unable to stop his tumble of words. Isaac gripped Penelope's hand hard. "What they said happened about your mum--"

"Dad!" Anthony shouted from across the room. The room fell quiet.

"We don't need to talk about that, dad...Anthony was perfectly clear when he requested we not talk about it..."

All of Isaac's insides felt wrong. His face was stoney and blank as he watched the exchange between the Mooren's. He saw the mortification in Penelope and Anthony's anger as they fought to quiet the family. Aunts and Uncles began to peek in through the kitchen, asking what the commotion was about.

"I'm taking Penelope to Paris," Isaac said abruptly. All eyes turned on him. "For her birthday. We won't miss the opportunity to see Paris when it's snowing."

"Oh how lovely," Rhonda beamed, grasping Isaac's hand, leaning in to give Penelope a kiss on the cheek.

The room buzzed with laughter and conversation once more specifically about the trip planned for Paris, but for Isaac, the only sound that mattered was Penelope's soft, joyful laugh beside the fire, her presence anchoring him in the midst of it all.

Later in the evening, as the younger children were sent off to bed and the adults lingered to sip on hot cocoa. Isaac found Anthony outside on the porch. The air was biting, their breath visible in soft puffs. Anthony leaned on the railing, gazing out at the snow-covered landscape, his features unreadable.

"Got a moment?" Isaac asked, stepping beside him.

Anthony nodded but didn't look at him. "You doing alright? It's a lot in there," he said, gesturing back toward the house.

Isaac chuckled lightly. "Yeah, it's a bit overwhelming. But your family's great."

They stood in silence for a moment, the sounds of laughter and music faint through the walls. Isaac clenched his fists in his coat pockets, trying to summon the courage to say what he needed to.

"Anthony," he began, his voice tentative. "There's something I've been thinking about. Something I wanted to talk to you about."

Anthony turned his head slightly, his expression curious.

Isaac took a deep breath, his words coming out in a rush. "I want to ask Penelope to marry me."

Anthony's brows shot up in surprise, but he didn't speak, so Isaac pushed on. "I know how much your dad cares about her. I know he's proud, and I know he'll never ask for help with the medical expenses, but I love her, Anthony. I really do. I want to take care of her, no matter what."

"That's generous but it's a lot to take on."

"Money isn't the problem," Isaac shook his head. "You know the wealth of my family."

"It's not that simple."

Anthony's jaw tightened, and he looked away, his hands gripping the railing. For a long moment, he didn't say anything, and Isaac felt a pit of dread forming in his stomach. Finally, Anthony exhaled shakily, his voice breaking.

"She's going to die, Isaac," Anthony said, his tone raw. "She's fought hard, but this isn't... it's not going to go away. And I can't—I can't just pretend everything's okay."

Isaac felt his throat tighten, but he stepped closer, his voice steady. "I know, Anthony. I know what the doctors have said, and I know what the odds are. But I still want to be there for her, for as long as she'll have me. I want to give her everything while I still can."

Anthony finally turned to face him, his eyes glistening with unshed tears. "Why?" he asked, his voice almost a whisper. "Why would you do this, knowing how it ends?"

Isaac swallowed hard. "Because I love her," he said simply. "And because she needs to be loved, to be cared for, not because she is dying, but because she deserves to have everything."

Anthony's shoulders shook, and he wiped at his eyes with the back of his hand. "You're a better man than I am," he said, his voice thick with emotion.

Anthony stepped forward, pulling Isaac into a brief, tight hug. When he pulled back, he nodded, his voice steadier. "Alright. If she says yes... I'll support you. Just—promise me you'll take care of her, Isaac. Promise me you'll make her happy."

"I promise," Isaac said, his voice firm.

Pulling away, Anthony made a face. "You need to talk to dad."

Isaac felt a weight in his chest as he ascended the creaking stairs to the attic of the Moorens' house. The air grew colder and heavier with each step, the faint scent of dust and old wood filling his nose. He hesitated briefly at the door, then stepped inside, finding Ray hunched over a stack of boxes, rifling through them with sharp, jerky movements.

"Having trouble?" Isaac asked, his voice cautious as he trailed his fingers along the edge of a dusty shelf.

Ray startled at the sound, standing bolt upright and knocking a box lid askew. His face was pale, his expression a mix of frustration and something deeper, something raw. "Isaac! I didn't hear you come up."

"Sorry, sir," Isaac said quickly, stepping further into the room. From downstairs, bursts of laughter floated faintly upward, a stark contrast to the charged silence of the attic. "Anthony mentioned you were up here."

"Yes, of course," Ray said, nodding absently. "What's on your mind? If it's about my comment earlier…"

Isaac shook his head. "Not at all."

"Good. Good." Ray turned back to the boxes, but his hands trembled as he resumed his search. His unease was palpable, each movement tense and distracted.

"Sir, are you alright?" Isaac asked carefully.

Ray let out a strained chuckle, though it sounded more like a sigh. "It's this attic. Just… so much clutter. Decades of odds and ends. What a mess."

"You're looking for your brother's record from university, right?" Isaac glanced at the nearest box. Instead of records, it held a collection of delicate keepsakes—lace bonnets, tiny socks, and faded ribbons. His hand hovered over them, but he stopped short, unwilling to disturb the fragile relics of the past.

Ray chuckled again, the sound hollow. "Yes, but it's the strangest thing. I can't find it anywhere."

Isaac hesitated, sensing the turmoil beneath Ray's distracted movements. "Mr. Mooren, I wanted to talk to you about something important. But if you're troubled, I'd like to help."

"Help." The word came out as a strained whisper. Ray turned away, biting his knuckles as he began to pace. His agitation was evident now, his movements erratic and uncharacteristic. "I'm at my wits' end, Isaac."

"You're worried," Isaac said softly, his throat tightening. "You're grieving a dying daughter."

Ray froze mid step. The words seemed to pierce through the fragile walls he'd built around himself. He sat heavily on a wooden crate, burying his face in his hands. Quiet sobs broke the stillness, muffled but deeply pained.

Isaac's chest tightened as he watched the man unravel. He stepped closer, placing a firm but gentle hand on Ray's quivering shoulder. The sounds of laughter and merriment from below felt like they belonged to another world entirely. Isaac lowered himself onto a crate across from Ray, waiting in silence as the man poured out his grief.

After a long moment, Ray's sobs quieted, leaving a heavy stillness in the air. He wiped his face with trembling hands, his voice rough as he spoke. "You are patient, Isaac. Listening to a tired old man weep."

"I'm no stranger to tears, sir," Isaac said gently. "Sometimes it's the only way to relieve the weight of what's truly grieving us."

Ray nodded slowly, his eyes red rimmed but steady. "Anthony speaks highly of you. Says you've had more than your share of hardship. I'm grateful for the care and friendship you've shown my little girl."

Isaac flushed, lowering his gaze briefly. "I love her, Mr. Mooren."

Ray let out a deep, resigned sigh. "Anthony was right."

Isaac offered a faint smile. "He probably bet on it." His expression turned serious. "I know how this ends, sir. I understand the outcome. But I refuse to stop loving her. Will you allow me to marry her?"

Ray's head shook almost imperceptibly. "That's a burden far too great for you. We've been scraping together funds for her treatments, but... my parents are getting older. We don't have that kind of money."

"It's not a burden," Isaac said after a moment's silence. "I want to marry her, Mr. Mooren. Few people know this, but my family has money. I have an inheritance, one that could ease the fears and hardships in the time we have left."

"I can't ask you to do this," Ray said, shaking his head again.

Isaac reached out, gripping the older man's hand firmly. "You're a proud man, Mr. Mooren. I've known my share of proud men. But even proud men need help. Would you refuse the kindness of the Samaritan, or would you turn away from the answer to your prayers?"

Ray stared at him, his jaw working as he struggled to form words. Finally, he whispered, "Nel told me you didn't believe in God."

Isaac smiled faintly, a trace of bitterness in his expression. "But you do, Mr. Mooren."

19

The air in Paris in February was crisp, with a biting chill softened by the allure of the city's eternal charm. Snow clung to the edges of rooftops and cobblestones, but the Seine flowed steadily, its waters reflecting the golden lights of streetlamps. Isaac tightened his scarf and glanced at Penelope, who walked beside him, her cheeks flushed from the cold. She wore a wool coat and a beret tilted at just the right angle, her delicate features illuminated by the glow of the Eiffel Tower in the distance.

"I still can't believe we're here," Penelope murmured, her voice soft but tinged with awe. She tilted her head back to take in the grandeur of the surrounding buildings, each one a masterpiece in its own right.

Isaac chuckled. "It feels surreal, doesn't it? Like stepping into a dream."

The days in Paris unfolded like a series of vivid, dreamlike moments. Each morning, the city welcomed Isaac and Penelope with its unique rhythm—a blend of quiet elegance and bustling vitality. The markets of Montmartre buzzed with life, the aroma of fresh baguettes and roasted chestnuts weaving through the air. Isaac marveled at Penelope's curiosity as she admired the stalls lined with vivid flowers, shimmering silks, and delicate pastries, her fingers brushing over the textures with a childlike wonder.

At the Luxembourg Gardens, they found serenity amidst perfectly trimmed hedges and grand fountains. Penelope took small but confident steps along the gravel paths, pausing to watch children sailing toy boats in the pond. The soft winter sun cast a golden glow over her face, and Isaac couldn't help but notice how the city seemed to suit her—as though Paris, in all its beauty and grace, had been waiting for her to arrive.

Afternoons were spent in cozy cafés, their tiny round tables barely big enough to hold their steaming cups of café au lait and delicate croissants. Penelope would lean back in her chair, her scarf loosely draped over her shoulders, recounting childhood memories or quoting lines from poetry that matched the romance of their surroundings. Isaac listened, captivated not just by her words but by the way her laughter rang out—light, melodic, and so unlike the weariness he had grown used to seeing in her.

At the Seine, they wandered through bookstores with creaking wooden floors and shelves that seemed to stretch endlessly upward. Isaac watched Penelope's fingers skim the spines of worn volumes, her eyes lighting up when she found something that caught her interest. He bought her a first edition of a French poetry collection, which she clutched to her chest like a treasure.

The Louvre was their last stop on one particular day, its grandeur unmatched. They strolled through echoing halls, marveling at the masterpieces. Penelope lingered longest before "The Winged Victory of Samothrace," her face unreadable as she took in the sculpture's poise and strength.

"It's like she's still moving forward," she whispered, almost to herself. Isaac squeezed her hand, silently agreeing.

One evening, the city seemed especially luminous, the lights reflecting off the Seine like scattered jewels. They stopped on a bridge, the chill of the night tempered by the beauty surrounding them. The faint hum of an accordion player reached them from a distant corner of the street.

The wind picked up, teasing Penelope's scarf until it slipped loose. Before it could sail away, Isaac's hand darted out, catching the edge of the soft fabric. He stepped closer, carefully draping it back around her neck, his movements slow and deliberate. His fingers brushed her jawline as he tucked the scarf into place, lingering for a moment longer than necessary.

Their eyes met, and for a moment, the city around them seemed to still. The Seine's gentle flow, the distant chatter of lovers strolling arm in arm, and even the cold air seemed to fade, leaving only the two of them in the warm glow of the bridge's lamplight.

"You make it hard to remember life before this," Isaac murmured, his voice barely louder than the breeze.

Penelope smiled, soft and wistful, her cheeks flushed. "Maybe that's the point," she replied, her words carrying the weight of both hope and fragility.

Isaac wanted to say more, to tell her how much she meant to him, how Paris seemed brighter because of her presence. But instead, he let the silence between them speak, his hand finding hers as they turned to watch the river together, the city's lights painting golden ripples on the water.

"Thank you for bringing me here," she said, her voice quiet but heartfelt.

"Thank you for coming with me," he replied, his tone equally earnest.

On their last night in the city, Isaac led Penelope to a small square tucked away from the bustling streets. A musician played a violin near a fountain, the hauntingly beautiful notes echoing through the air. Snowflakes began to fall, delicate and soft, dusting their hair and coats.

Isaac held out his hand. "Dance with me?"

Penelope hesitated, her brows raising in playful surprise. "Here? In the middle of the square?"

He nodded, his expression serious but hopeful. "Here. Right now."

She smiled, shaking her head lightly but placing her hand in his. Isaac pulled her close, his arm wrapping around her waist as they swayed to the music. Her body was light against his, her head resting briefly on his chest as they moved together. The rest of the world faded away—no tourists, no passersby, no city, no illness. Just the two of them, dancing under the soft glow of Parisian street lights.

As they stood on that bridge, the city's lights casting a soft, warm glow over the Seine, Isaac turned to Penelope, his heart heavy but resolute. He took her hands in his, feeling their warmth, and took a deep breath before he spoke.

"Penelope," he began, his voice steady, "I've thought about this moment a thousand times, and I knew that I wanted to be here with you, now. To ask you…" He paused, his eyes searching hers as though looking for a sign that she was ready to hear him.

"I love you more than anything," he continued, his words coming from a place of certainty and a fierce protectiveness. "I know that your life isn't the same as it was, but I want you to know that I'm here to take care of you—now, through every moment, and especially in your final days."

He took another step closer, his hands tightening around hers as he looked into her eyes. "I want to be there for you, every step of the way," he said softly, his voice unwavering. "I want to be the one who makes you laugh when it feels like nothing can anymore, who helps you find joy in the little things, even when everything else seems so dark."

His grip tightened, his voice breaking just slightly. "Penelope, I want to spend my life with you, no matter how long that might be. I want to make your final days as full of love and peace as I can. Will you marry me?"

Tears shimmered in her eyes as she looked up at him, her hands squeezing his back. "Isaac," she whispered, her voice thick with emotion. "Yes, I will marry you."

Isaac pulled her into his arms, holding her tightly, knowing that this was just the beginning of a journey they would face together, no matter how difficult it might be. "I promise," he murmured against her hair, "to take care of you, to make every day count. We'll face whatever comes next, together."

Later that night, back at the apartment, they sat by the fire, their fingers intertwined. Penelope traced the band of the ring on her finger, her smile soft and content. Isaac watched her, his heart full, then took a deep breath.

"There's something I want to tell you," he said, breaking the quiet.

Penelope turned to him, her brows lifting in curiosity. "What is it?"

"I've been thinking," Isaac began, his voice careful but resolute. "If we're going to get married, I want to do it right. I want to be baptized so we can be married in the church."

Penelope blinked, her expression shifting from surprise to something more profound—an almost reverent kind of gratitude. "Isaac... you don't have to do that for me."

"I know," he said quickly. "This isn't just for you—it's for us. I want to do this because it feels right. I want to share everything with you, Penelope. My life, my faith, my heart. All of it."

Tears welled in her eyes again, but she smiled, leaning forward to cup his face in her hands. "You have no idea how much that means to me."

Isaac covered her hands with his, his gaze steady. "Then it's settled. When we get home, I'll start the process."

They sat together in the quiet warmth of the firelight, the city outside buzzing with life. Isaac held Penelope close.

20

As the morning sun streamed through the stained glass windows of the cathedral, casting colorful patterns on the polished stone floor, Isaac stood in front of the full-length mirror, adjusting his dark suit. Malcom, hovered nearby, a steady presence as he helped Isaac with the final touches.

Malcom's hands were steady as he adjusted the collar of Isaac's white dress shirt, his fingers moving carefully. "You look good, Isaac," he murmured, his voice low and comforting. "Penelope's going to be blown away."

Isaac offered a weak smile, feeling the weight of the day settling heavily on his shoulders. "I hope so," he replied, his voice tight with nerves. "It's a big deal, isn't it?"

"It is," Malcom agreed, his eyes softening. "But you've waited for this moment, Isaac. She's going to be so happy when she sees you."

Anthony stood quietly in the corner of the room, watching as Malcom helped Isaac adjust his tie. His expression was thoughtful, his eyes never straying too far from Isaac's reflection. "She's lucky to have you, Isaac," he said finally, his tone gentle.

Isaac's hands hesitated for a moment as he pulled the tie tight around his neck. "I just want to make her happy," he admitted, his voice breaking. "To be enough for her."

"You are enough, Isaac," Anthony said firmly. "And more. Penelope's lucky to have someone who cares about her the way you do."

Malcom stepped back once Isaac's tie was perfectly in place, giving him a final once-over. "You're ready," he said, his smile wide and genuine. "Ready to marry the love of your life."

Isaac took a deep breath, nodding his thanks. "Thanks, both of you," he said, his voice steadying. "I wouldn't be here without you."

The three men left the room, descending the grand staircase to the church entrance. The doors swung open, revealing the breathtaking interior of the cathedral, pews lined with friends and family, the air heavy with the scent of roses and polished wood. It was a sea of people in formal wear, the guests chatting quietly as they waited for the ceremony to begin.

Isaac felt his heart speed up as they walked towards the front, his steps steady but his hands trembling. The music began to play, soft and lilting, signaling the start of the ceremony. Penelope's entrance was marked by a murmur through the crowd in a hush that spread like ripples across a pond.

Isaac's eyes fixed on the aisle, watching as Penelope, radiant in a white gown, walked towards him on her father's arm. Her hair was swept up, the veil gently cascading down her back. Her eyes were fixed on Isaac's, a smile on her face that was both nervous and filled with love.

When they finally reached the altar, Penelope's father kissed her cheek and stepped back, leaving her standing beside Isaac. Her hand trembled slightly as she took his, their fingers intertwining as the priest began the ceremony.

The words were familiar, vows of love, promises of fidelity and care, but Isaac heard each one with a clarity he had never felt before. His gaze never wavered from Penelope's face as he listened, his heart swelling with the love he felt for her.

When it was time to exchange rings, Isaac fumbled slightly with the delicate band, slipping it onto Penelope's finger. She smiled up at him, her eyes bright with tears, and slid the matching ring onto his hand.

The priest's final words were a blessing, and when he pronounced them husband and wife, Isaac could barely believe it. The kiss was a moment of pure joy, Isaac's hands sliding around Penelope's waist as they leaned in, their lips meeting softly. It was brief, but it felt like a lifetime of promises made in one simple kiss.

As they walked back down the aisle together, the guests erupted in applause, the sound deafening in the echoing cathedral. Isaac's arm tightened around Penelope's waist, his heart pounding as they made their way to the front of the church for photographs and well-wishes.

Malcom and Anthony joined them, clapping Isaac on the back with broad smiles. "Congrats, mate," Anthony said, his eyes shining with pride. "You really did it."

Isaac's throat was tight with emotion as he pulled Penelope close, pressing a kiss to her temple. "Worth every second," he whispered to her.

PART FOUR

21

March 1999.

The pub was dimly lit, the warm glow of the stage lights casting long shadows across the small, intimate space. Isaac was in his element, his guitar slung low across his chest as he swayed with the beat of the music. The crowd was buzzing, their voices blending with the melody, laughter interspersed with the sound of clinking glasses.

Penelope was at the front of the small audience, her eyes fixed on Isaac as he played. She was smiling, her fingers tapping lightly against the table in time with the music. Isaac could feel the energy of the room rising with every chord he played, the connection between him and the audience electric.

He lost himself in the music, the words flowing from his lips with ease, his fingers dancing across the strings of his guitar. It was a perfect moment, one that Isaac knew he would remember forever. Penelope's gaze was a constant presence, a beacon of light in the dark room, and it gave him the strength to keep going, to pour every ounce of himself into his performance.

When the last note of the song drifted away, there was applause, loud and heartfelt. Isaac took a deep breath, offering a grateful smile to the crowd as he took a step back from the mic. The room seemed to swell with energy, the sound of clapping and cheers rising up around him.

Isaac made his way through the crowd, a few fans reaching out to shake his hand or offer compliments on his performance. Penelope was waiting for him by the exit, her smile wide and bright as she stepped forward to meet him. "You were amazing," she said, her voice full of warmth. "Absolutely perfect."

He leaned down to kiss her, his hands settling on her waist as he pulled her close. "Thank you," he murmured against her lips, his eyes searching hers. "I'm glad you liked it."

Penelope wrapped her arms around his neck, holding on tight. "Of course I liked it," she replied, her smile never fading.

As they walked out of the pub together, the sound of the music fading behind them, Isaac felt lighter than he had in months. They headed back to the Mooren house, the night cool and clear, the stars twinkling above them. Penelope was humming softly to herself, her head resting against Isaac's shoulder as they walked.

When they arrived home, the house was quiet. The Mooren's had gone to bed hours earlier, leaving only Isaac and Penelope to their own devices. Penelope was still smiling as they entered the kitchen, setting down her guitar case with a soft thud.

Isaac's smile faltered as he noticed the way Penelope's energy seemed to sag slightly, her movements slower than usual. "You feeling okay?" he asked, his brow furrowing with concern.

Penelope nodded, but the gesture was weak. "Just a little tired," she said, her voice barely above a whisper. "I'll be fine."

But Isaac wasn't convinced. "Come on," he said gently, guiding her to the couch in the living room. "Let's get you something to drink, huh?"

He fetched a glass of water from the kitchen, bringing it back to her as she sank onto the cushions. Penelope took a sip, her fingers trembling slightly as she set the glass back down. "I'm okay," she insisted, her smile wavering. "Just a bit worn out."

Isaac wasn't so sure. He watched her closely, noting the way she seemed to sway slightly even when she was sitting still. "Let's get you up to bed," he suggested, his voice low and steady. "You need rest."

Penelope's eyes were starting to close, her head drooping forward. "Isaac..." she murmured, her voice fading.

Panic shot through Isaac's chest. "Penelope? Hey, stay with me," he said, his voice sharp with urgency. "Penelope!"

She didn't respond, her head hanging loosely. Isaac's heart was pounding as he reached out, gripping her shoulders gently. "Penelope, wake up," he said, his voice steady but panicked. "Come on, sweetheart."

When she still didn't move, Isaac's mind raced. Shouting for her to wake up. He heard creaking from upstairs, as someone came down the steps in a great hurry. Mr. Mooren looked wide-eyed in his night clothes, his dressing gown draped haphazardly over his shoulders. Isaac was breathless, quickly taking Penelope in his arms.

"What's happened?" he demanded, his voice sharp.

"She's not waking up," Isaac said, his voice thick with fear. "We need to get her to the hospital. Now!"

Mr. Mooren didn't hesitate, they were out into the chill night air, the car roaring to life as they sped through the streets of their small town. Isaac held Penelope's hand in the backseat, his heart lodged in his throat as he tried to keep her awake, talking to her softly, begging her to stay with him.

The hospital was a blur of lights and noise when they arrived, the emergency entrance illuminated by harsh fluorescent lights. Isaac jumped out of the car before it even came to a complete stop, scooping Penelope up in his arms and running towards the sliding doors. Mr. Mooren followed closely behind, yelling for help.

Isaac's legs felt like lead as he carried Penelope through the sterile hallways, the sharp scent of antiseptic filling his nose. He felt detached, numb—he could hardly believe what was happening. "Help!" he shouted again, his voice hoarse with panic. "Please, someone help us!"

Nurses appeared from around a corner, their expressions grim as they took Penelope from Isaac's arms. He felt the world tilt beneath him as they rushed her away, disappearing through a set of double doors.

Isaac dropped to his knees, his hands trembling as he tried to steady himself.

"Isaac?" Mr. Moore's voice was heavy with concern as he knelt beside Isaac, his hand on his shoulder. "She's going to be okay," he said, his tone more hopeful than Isaac felt. "They're going to fix her."

Isaac couldn't speak, he could only nod, the tears burning in his eyes as he watched the doors close behind Penelope. He felt as if he were standing on the edge of a cliff, everything around him crumbling.

"We'll wait," Mr. Mooren said softly, his voice steady and strong. "Together."

Isaac closed his eyes, taking deep breaths as he tried to find a way to keep his hope alive, to believe that Penelope would be okay. The waiting began then, a silent vigil in the hospital lobby, every minute stretching into eternity.

22

The hospital was a sterile, clinical world where every corner seemed to echo with the weight of countless worries and fears. For Isaac, it was a place of bittersweet memories, where life and death seemed to be separated by the thinnest of lines. Penelope remained in the hospital, her condition fragile after contracting an infection. Isaac visited her every day, a ritual that gave him solace in the midst of uncertainty.

The first time Isaac walked through the automatic sliding doors, he felt a cold draft against his face. The entrance was bustling with activity, the constant coming and going of nurses, doctors, and patients. Isaac's eyes searched the familiar white and blue signage, looking for the way to the intensive care unit where Penelope was being treated. He took a deep breath, his hands trembling slightly, and moved forward, determination etched across his face.

The intensive care unit was as cold as it was quiet, a far cry from the bustling world Isaac had just stepped out of. The room was dimly lit, the walls painted a muted beige that did little to break the monotony of the medical equipment and monitors. Penelope's bed was surrounded by tubes and wires, every beeping sound of the machines an unnerving reminder of her condition. Isaac's heart clenched as he approached the bedside, his eyes tracing every line of Penelope's pale face.

"Hey," he whispered, his voice breaking as he leaned down to press a kiss to her forehead. Penelope's eyes fluttered open, a weak smile forming on her lips when she saw him. "Hey," she managed, her voice barely audible.

Isaac's heart swelled with relief. He took her hand in his, squeezing it gently. "How are you feeling today?" he asked, his voice soft, the worry clear in his eyes.

"Better," Penelope replied, though there was a hint of hesitation in her voice. "They're giving me antibiotics now, trying to fight off the infection."

Isaac nodded, brushing a loose strand of hair from her forehead. "I brought you something," he said, his voice thick with emotion as he reached into his bag. He pulled out a small bouquet of flowers, lilies and daisies, bright and cheerful, despite the hospital's stark surroundings.

Penelope's eyes lit up as she took the flowers from him, bringing them close to her face to breathe in their scent. "They're beautiful," she said softly, her fingers brushing against Isaac's as she set the flowers on the bedside table. "Thank you."

Isaac smiled, the relief of seeing her smile making his own heartache a little less sharp. "Of course," he replied, his voice steady as he pulled up a chair beside her bed. "I thought you might like some company."

Penelope reached for his hand, her fingers curling around his. "You're always here," she said, her voice breaking slightly. "You don't have to be, you know."

Isaac shook his head, squeezing her hand gently. "I want to be here," he said firmly. "You're my whole world, Penelope. I'm not going anywhere."

They spent the next hour together, Isaac reading from a well-worn copy of Hamlet, his voice soothing as he delivered the lines with emotion. Penelope listened quietly, a small smile on her lips as he recited the speeches, bringing Shakespeare's words to life in a way that only he could.

When he finished, Penelope squeezed his hand gently. "Thank you," she said softly, her voice steady. "For being here. For everything."

Isaac leaned down, pressing a kiss to her forehead. "I'll always be here," he promised, his voice low and sincere. "No matter what happens."

After that, Isaac brought his guitar with him whenever he visited. He would find a quiet corner of the hospital, a hallway, a waiting area, even the cafeteria where he could sit and play for her. He'd play their favorite songs, the ones that reminded them of nights spent on rooftops, watching the stars, or dancing in the kitchen as the radio played. The music was a gift, an escape from the sterile world of beeping monitors and sterile sheets.

The nurses would sometimes gather, leaning against walls or sitting on chairs, listening with soft smiles as Isaac poured his heart into his guitar. Penelope would close her eyes, her head resting against the pillow, a small tear escaping from the corner of her eye as she listened.

It was in those moments that Isaac could almost believe everything would be okay.

One day, after playing a particularly tender ballad, Isaac noticed Penelope's eyes were closed longer than usual. She was breathing softly, her fingers still holding his. Isaac's heart clenched, fear rising in his chest. "Penelope?" he called softly, his voice breaking. "Penelope, wake up."

There was no response.

Isaac's breath hitched as he leaned closer, his fingers brushing against her face. "Penelope, come on, wake up," he urged, his voice cracking. "Please, stay with me."

A nurse appeared at the doorway, her expression urgent. "Sir, we need to check her vitals," she said gently, moving past Isaac to check the monitors around Penelope's bed.

Isaac's heart was pounding as he watched the nurse work, his body numb with fear. "Is she okay?" he asked, his voice barely a whisper.

The nurse hesitated, her eyes meeting Isaac's for a moment before she turned back to the monitors. "We're checking her now," she replied softly. "I'll let you know as soon as we know something."

Isaac nodded, his hands trembling as he reached out to touch Penelope's arm. "Come on," he whispered, his voice breaking. "Stay with me."

Penelope didn't wake up for the rest of the day. Isaac stayed by her side, holding her hand, talking to her softly as if that could bring her back to him. He brought flowers again, roses this time, bright red and full of life, just like Penelope had always been. He set them on the bedside table and sat down beside her, his fingers tracing patterns on her hand as he whispered his love to her over and over again.

When Mr. Mooren arrived in the evening, Isaac barely looked up. The older man's eyes were red-rimmed, his face drawn with worry. He didn't say anything, just sat down beside Isaac, wrapping an arm around his shoulders in a silent show of support.

Together, they watched the monitors, the beeping sounds a constant reminder of Penelope's struggle. Isaac's gaze stayed fixed on her, his heart aching with every breath he saw her take.

As the night wore on, Penelope's condition stabilized slightly. The nurse returned to give Isaac the news, Penelope was still weak, but the infection was starting to respond to the antibiotics. Isaac felt a wave of relief wash over him, his eyes closing as he took a deep breath.

"She's going to be okay," he murmured, more to himself than to anyone else. Mr. Mooren nodded, squeezing Isaac's shoulder gently.

For the first time in days, Isaac allowed himself to believe it, to believe that they might leave the hospital together. The road ahead would be difficult, he knew, but he was willing to walk it. For Penelope.

That night, he sat beside her bed, holding her hand as he drifted off to sleep. The room was quiet, just the soft sound of the machines and the occasional footsteps of nurses in the hallway. Isaac's dreams were restless, filled with shadows and whispers, but he held on to the memory of Penelope's smile believing that as long as she was there, they could face anything together.

23

Isaac sat in the dimly lit hospital room, his fingers brushing gently over the strings of his guitar. The soft, melancholic melody filled the air, weaving through the sterile, white-walled space like a whispered promise. Penelope lay in the bed, her face serene in sleep, her breathing shallow but steady. The monitors beeped softly, a reminder of the fragile hold she still had on life.

Isaac's heart ached as he played, each note a prayer, each strum a wish for her recovery. He closed his eyes, letting the music carry away his fears and doubts. Penelope had always found solace in his music, something that had always grounded her during her darkest moments. Isaac kept his voice low as he sang softly along with the song, his eyes flicking occasionally to Penelope's peaceful face.

When he finished, Isaac gently placed the guitar on the bedside table and pulled a chair closer to Penelope. He reached out to brush a lock of hair away from her forehead, his touch as tender as he could manage. "I'm here, Penelope," he whispered, his voice breaking. "Always."

He watched her for a moment longer, his heart in his throat, then stood and quietly left the room, trying to keep the walls from closing in around him. The hallways were quiet, the lights overhead casting long shadows along the linoleum floor. Isaac moved through the sterile, quiet corridor, his footsteps muted as he made his way to the small, cramped office where the doctors and nurses took their breaks.

Pushing open the door, Isaac found himself face to face with a small group of medical staff, a nurse checking charts, a doctor on the phone, and a young intern looking through a clipboard. The office was warm in contrast to the cool hospital halls, and Isaac took a deep breath, hoping the air would clear his thoughts.

"Excuse me," he said softly, catching the attention of the nurse who looked up with a nod. "Can I—can I talk to the doctor for a moment?"

The nurse gave him a sympathetic smile. "Of course, Isaac," she said gently. "Doctor Adair is on a call right now, but he should be done soon."

Isaac nodded and stepped into the room, leaning against the doorframe. The sound of Penelope's name was barely audible through the thin walls, and Isaac's heart twisted with worry. He closed his eyes and took another deep breath, focusing on the rhythm of his breathing to steady himself.

After what felt like an eternity, the door opened, and Doctor Adair stepped through, his phone tucked into his coat pocket. His expression was grave as he looked at Isaac, no words needed to be said. "Isaac," he greeted softly, giving a small nod. "I understand you have some questions about Penelope?"

Isaac forced a smile, though it didn't reach his eyes. "How is she, really?"

Doctor Adair hesitated, then looked down at the floor before meeting Isaac's gaze again. "She's responding to the antibiotics," he said slowly. "But she's still very weak. We need to monitor her closely, but it takes time."

Isaac nodded, his fingers curling into fists at his sides. "Can—can I ask you something?" he asked, his voice catching slightly. "About—about the time she has left?"

Doctor Adair hesitated, his eyes flicking over Isaac's face as if searching for something. "We're doing everything we can," he said gently. "But I need you to prepare yourself for the possibility that—" He broke off, unable to say the words.

"I know," Isaac interrupted, his voice steady despite the terror in his eyes. "I just—can you—can you give me a time? Weeks, months?"

Doctor Adair took a deep breath, his eyes fixed on Isaac. "It's hard to say," he admitted. "It could be weeks, or it could be sooner. We just don't know."

Isaac nodded, trying to keep his emotions in check. "Thank you," he said quietly. "I—appreciate your honesty."

The doctor gave him a small, understanding smile. "Anytime," he replied, his gaze lingering for a moment before he stepped back. "If you need anything, just let me know."

Isaac watched him leave, his shoulders slumping as the door closed behind the doctor. He felt a hand on his shoulder and turned to find Anthony standing there, his eyes red-rimmed and pained.

"Isaac," Anthony said softly, his voice breaking. "How is she?"

Isaac looked away, his eyes burning with unshed tears. "Not good," he admitted, his voice barely a whisper. "They're saying—weeks, maybe months."

Anthony's face crumpled, and he pulled Isaac into a tight hug. "Fuck," he whispered, his voice thick with emotion.

Isaac buried his face in Anthony's shoulder, feeling the warmth and strength of his friend's embrace. "I just—" Isaac choked out, his voice breaking. "I just want to take care of her."

"I know you do," Anthony replied, his voice steady, though Isaac could hear the tears in his tone. "And you will. You're the best thing that's ever happened to her, Isaac. Don't forget that."

They stood there in the corridor for a long moment, clinging to each other as if their combined strength could keep Penelope safe. Isaac felt the world tilt on its axis, the fear and the heartbreak almost overwhelming. But with Anthony's arms around him, Isaac knew he wasn't alone.

"I love her," Isaac finally said, his voice steady, despite the tears. "I just—I want to make every moment count."

"I know," Anthony replied, his voice thick with emotion. "And you will. Penelope's lucky to have you."

They held each other for a moment longer, the warmth of their embrace a lifeline in the cold hospital hallway. Then, with a deep breath, Isaac pulled away, his eyes determined. "I need to go back in," he said quietly, his voice steady.

"Go," Anthony urged, giving him a small push toward the door. "She's waiting for you."

24

Isaac sat in the rehearsal hall, his fingers drumming absentmindedly on his knee as he tried to focus on Thomas going through his lines. The fluorescent lights overhead buzzed softly, casting an oppressive glow over the room. The rest of the cast was lost in their roles, projecting their emotions across the space, but Isaac's mind felt a thousand miles away. His eyes kept drifting to the clock on the wall, counting down the minutes until the end of practice.

Thomas's voice broke through Isaac's distracted thoughts. "Isaac, are you with us?" he asked, his brow furrowed with concern.

Isaac blinked, tearing his gaze away from the clock. "Yeah," he mumbled, nodding absently. "Sorry, just—distracted."

Thomas stepped closer, his expression sympathetic. "You can tell me anything, Isaac." He said quietly, lowering his voice as the rest of the cast continued rehearsing around them.

Isaac hesitated, then shook his head. "It's nothing," he lied, forcing a smile. "Just a long day."

Thomas studied him for a moment longer, then gave a slow nod. "Okay, but if you ever need to talk—"

"I know," Isaac cut in, grateful for the offer but not willing to burden his friend. "Thanks, really."

With a final, concerned glance, Thomas returned to his place among the cast, continuing his lines with a renewed energy. Isaac turned his attention back to the rehearsal, but the words and movements on stage seemed distant, detached. He couldn't concentrate on the lines or the blocking; all he could think about was how restless he felt, how his skin itched with the need to move.

The rain was pouring outside by the time practice ended, a thick, gray drizzle that seemed to match Isaac's mood. He lingered in the empty hall, watching the droplets race down the windows, tracing patterns in the condensation. It wasn't until the last cast member left, calling a quick goodbye over their shoulder, that Isaac finally pushed himself up and left the building.

The streets were slick with rain, the sound of it pounding on the pavement filling Isaac's ears as he walked, his hands shoved deep into the pockets of his jeans. He barely noticed the cold, too lost in his thoughts as he made his way through the city, the shadows of the buildings looming overhead. Every step felt heavy, like he was walking through mud.

He turned a corner and found himself beneath an overpass, the noise of the traffic above muffled by the concrete walls. Isaac hesitated for a moment, then walked on, his boots sloshing in the puddles. There was someone else under the bridge, a man huddled in a threadbare coat, a small, tattered satchel clutched in his lap.

"Hey," Isaac called softly, his voice low to avoid startling the man. "You got the message?"

The man looked up, his eyes sharp in the dim light. "Yeah," he replied, his voice low and gravelly. "You got what I need?"

Isaac hesitated, his fingers brushing against the small baggie in his pocket. He knew what was inside, had bought it on impulse earlier in the day, but now he wasn't sure if he could go through with it. "Yeah," he said, his voice steady. "I got it."

The man reached into his coat and pulled out a small, beat-up phone, tapping it a few times before holding it up to Isaac. On the screen was a simple message: Just a taste.

Isaac nodded, his throat tight as he turned away, walking back out into the rain. He could feel the eyes of the man on his back, watching as he disappeared into the shadows. It wasn't until he was halfway down the street that Isaac dared to slip his hand back into his pocket, feeling the small baggie there, safe and untouched.

He walked for hours, letting the rain soak through his jacket, the chill grounding him in a way he couldn't explain. The darkness of the city seemed to close in around him, the weight of the world pressing down on his shoulders. But every time he thought about reaching for that baggie, Isaac remembered the look in Penelope's eyes, the way she had smiled at him the last time he saw her.

By the time he found himself standing outside the hospital, Isaac's head was clearer, his steps more steady. He looked up at the building, the lights inside casting a warm, welcoming glow in the gloom of the night. For a moment, he hesitated, his fingers brushing over the pocket where the baggie still sat, then he turned away, walking back into the hospital with a new determination.

When he got to Penelope's room, he found her awake, her eyes bleary but focused as she watched him approach. Isaac took a deep breath, forcing a smile. "Hey," he said softly, his voice steady. "How's my girl doing?"

Penelope's eyes softened as she reached out for his hand. "Just a little better," she said, her voice weak but steady. "You're late tonight."

Isaac sat beside her, taking her hand in his. "Yeah, got caught up at practice," he admitted, squeezing her fingers gently. "But I'm here now."

She smiled, her grip tightening on his hand. "Good," she said softly. "I missed you."

"I missed you too," Isaac replied, his heart heavy with the fear and the love he felt for her. "Didn't get you any flowers today, though."

Penelope chuckled, her laughter small and tired. "That's okay," she said, leaning her head back against the pillow. "Just glad you're here."

"Always," Isaac murmured, his thumb brushing across her knuckles. "I wrote you something." Pulling out his guitar, he sat nearest to her.

25

The air in the hospital room was heavy, thick with the scent of antiseptic and the muffled sounds of monitors beeping in the background. Isaac sat by Penelope's side, holding her hand, his fingers tracing the lines of her palm as if trying to memorize her touch. Her once-vibrant eyes were now dimmed with fatigue and pain, the light behind them fading fast.

The soft beeping of the machines seemed to echo louder than the silence around them. Penelope lay still in the bed, her breath shallow and labored. Isaac's heart felt like it was being squeezed tighter with each beat. He had never been one to believe in fate, but as he watched her fade away, he couldn't help but think that maybe it was all just too cruel.

"Isaac," Penelope whispered, her voice barely above a whisper, her eyes fluttering open. Her gaze was clouded, searching for something. Isaac leaned closer, brushing a lock of hair from her forehead.

"I'm here, Pen," he whispered back, his voice cracking. "I'm right here."

She tried to smile, her lips curving weakly. "I knew you'd come back. I knew you'd find me." She was fading, her eyes moving back and fourth.

Just then, the door creaked open, and a nurse entered, her steps slow and deliberate. She carried a stack of papers in her hands, her face lined with concern. Isaac looked up, his breath hitching.

"Mr. Maison?" the nurse said gently, her voice breaking through his haze of emotion. "I've been waiting for you. I have something for you."

Isaac wiped his eyes and stood, brushing the tears away. "What is it?"

The nurse approached, handing him the stack of papers. "I was with Penelope earlier today when she was... lucid," she began, her voice low and sympathetic. "She asked me to write a letter for you."

Isaac's heart sank. "A letter?"

The nurse nodded, her gaze soft. "She wanted you to have it. She said it was important."

Tears pricked at Isaac's eyes as he took the letter, feeling the weight of it in his hands. He hesitated, looking back at Penelope, who was now staring at the ceiling, lost in thought.

"Can I..." Isaac choked out, his voice barely a whisper. "Can I read it now?"

The nurse nodded again, stepping back to give him space. Isaac took a deep breath, then turned his focus back to the letter. His hands shook as he opened it.

My dearest, the letter began. *If you're reading this, it means I didn't make it. I want you to know how much you meant to me, how much I loved you. These past few months have been the happiest of my life because I had you by my side.* Isaac's throat tightened as he read the words, his eyes blurring further. *I love you. I have loved you since the moment I nearly broke your nose at roller disco. Even in New York I couldn't imagine being with anyone but you.* Tears spilled over, and Isaac's breath hitched as he choked back a sob. *You gave me life again, when I thought all hope of happiness was gone forever. I love you, dearest of all that brings joy, thank you for giving me your heart. You will always have mine. Don't regret my loss, find your heart again. I love you forever.*

Isaac's vision blurred with tears as he folded the letter carefully, slipping it into his pocket. Penelope was slipping away, her body weaker by the second. He looked back at her, his heart breaking at the thought of never hearing her voice again, never feeling her touch.

"Please," Isaac whispered, his voice cracking. "Don't leave me."

The monitor beeped faster, the sound growing more urgent. Isaac's grip on Penelope's hand tightened as he felt the tears overwhelm him. He leaned forward, resting his forehead against hers. Penelope's hand went limp in his. The monitors went flat, the beeping abruptly stopping. Isaac closed his eyes, feeling the weight of her loss settle over him like a shroud.

He stayed there for what felt like hours, holding her hand, lost in the silence of the hospital room. The door creaked open again, and Anthony appeared in the doorway, his eyes red, his face streaked with tears.

"Isaac," he said softly, his voice breaking. "She's gone."

26

The door to the flat creaked open, revealing the dimly lit hallway beyond. Isaac stepped inside, feeling the weight of the day pressing down on him. Malcom followed closely behind, closing the door softly behind him. The apartment was quiet, a stark contrast to the bustling atmosphere of the hospital.

Isaac's gaze flickered around the familiar space, his eyes scanning the rooms as if looking for some semblance of comfort that just wasn't there. It was a place that had once been filled with laughter and warmth, now empty, suffused with a hollow silence.

Malcom moved to the living room, finding a place to sit on the threadbare couch. Isaac hesitated, lingering near the doorway, his hands shoved deep into his pockets. The corners of his eyes felt heavy with unshed tears, his throat tight with unspeakable sorrow.

Anthony had gone back to his parents' place to help them prepare for their move to Holland. Isaac knew it was for the best, they needed the support now more than ever. But it left him alone, a void in the flat that seemed to echo with every step he took.

"Isaac…" Malcom's voice was soft, his concern palpable. "You should talk to him."

Isaac shook his head, avoiding Malcom's eyes. "I can't…"

Malcolm stood, crossing the room slowly until he was standing in front of Isaac. "Why not? It's not his fault, Isaac. He's grieving too."

Isaac's jaw clenched as he turned away, focusing on the empty hallway beyond. "I know it's not his fault, Malcom. But I feel like it is. I feel… lost."

Malcom's hand landed gently on Isaac's shoulder, giving it a re-assuring squeeze. "You're not lost. You're just… hurting. It's okay to hurt."

Isaac turned back, his eyes clouded with pain. "How can I be okay with this? How can I just go on?"

"You take it day by day," Malcom said, his voice firm but compassionate. "You don't have to be okay right now."

Isaac's lip quivered, his eyes tearing up. "I don't know if I can."

Malcom pulled him into a hug, squeezing tightly as Isaac's breath hitched. "You can, Isaac. I know you can."

The moment stretched out between them, Malcom's presence grounding Isaac in a way that nothing else seemed to. They stood there for a long time, just holding each other, the world outside fading away.

Finally, Isaac pulled back, wiping his eyes with the back of his hand. "I can't keep running, Malcom. I can't keep hiding from it."

Malcom's eyes softened, his hand resting on Isaac's shoulder. "Then don't. You don't have to run anymore. You can face it. You've got people who love you, who want to help you."

Isaac nodded, taking a deep breath. "I know. I just… I don't know how."

"Start by letting people in," Malcom suggested, his tone gentle. "Don't shut them out, Isaac. You're not alone."

Isaac looked down, his fingers fumbling with the buttons on his jacket. "Anthony's not even here. He's helping his parents move. And I... I can't even look at him."

Malcom's gaze softened. "He knows you're hurting, Isaac. And he's hurting too. You need to let him know you're not blaming him."

Isaac swallowed hard, feeling the lump in his throat grow heavier.

"Then do it when you're ready," Malcom said softly. "But don't let this distance come between you two forever."

"I'll try." Isaac nodded, feeling the weight of the world on his shoulders. "I just... need to be alone for a bit."

"Take all the time you need," Malcom replied, understanding in his eyes.

Isaac nodded again, giving a small, broken smile. "Thanks, Mal."

Malcom gave him one final pat on the shoulder before heading towards the door. "I'll be right downstairs if you need me."

As the door closed behind Malcom, Isaac turned slowly, his steps heavy as he walked towards his room. The flat seemed impossibly empty without Penelope's laughter, her voice, the sound of her footsteps moving through the rooms.

Isaac's breath caught as he reached into his pocket, feeling the small baggie that had been weighing him down for weeks. He pulled it out, holding it in his palm, staring at it as if it were a stranger's. His heart pounded as he glared at it, the remnants of his old life, the temptation that had been haunting him.

"I can't," he whispered, his voice breaking. "I can't do this to her memory."

With a shuddering breath, Isaac closed his hand around the baggie and then shoved it deep into his pocket. He sank onto his bed, burying his face in his hands, tears slipping through his fingers.

"I'm sorry, Penelope," he murmured, the words barely audible. "I promised you…"

27

I saac's hands shook as he made his way through the back entrance of the theater. The fluorescent lights above flickered intermittently, casting long shadows across the narrow hallway. He was late, late to his own performance, late to the opening night of the play he had been rehearsing for months. But now, standing just outside the dressing rooms, Isaac hesitated.

His heart was racing, his chest tight. The air was thick with anxiety, the weight of everything he had been through pressing down on him. Penelope's face flashed through his mind, the sight of her lying in that hospital bed, her eyes closed, her body frail and weak. It felt like a weight had settled on his shoulders, the burden too heavy to bear.

"Isaac?" Neil's voice was a low rumble in the quiet hallway, his footsteps echoing as he approached. "You okay?"

Isaac turned slowly, his eyes red, his expression distant. "I… I don't think I can do this, Neil."

Neil's brows furrowed, his concern etched across his face. "What do you mean? This is your moment, Isaac. You've worked for this."

"It's not right," Isaac said, his voice tight. "I can't go on. It's not right without Penelope here."

Neil reached out, placing a hand on Isaac's shoulder.

Isaac clenched his jaw, his hands curling into fists. "I can't... I can't focus. I can't even think straight."

Neil took a step closer, his voice calm and steady. "Then let's take a breath, alright? Let's just... take a step back."

Isaac nodded, the weight of his emotions pulling him down. He turned away, needing a moment to gather himself. The dressing room was only a few steps away, and he stumbled toward it, his legs feeling heavy with the burden of his panic.

He closed the door behind him, leaning against it as he tried to steady his breathing. His heart was pounding in his ears, the sound of it almost drowning out everything else. The room was dimly lit, the mirror above the sink casting a shadow over his reflection.

"I can't do this," he muttered to himself, his hands shaking as he reached up to undo his jacket. The fabric felt tight, suffocating against his skin.

As he pulled the jacket off, the little baggie fell from his pocket, landing on the floor with a soft thud. Isaac froze, his eyes locking onto it. The sight of the small, clear packet of white felt like a betrayal—his old self, still haunting him, still tempting him.

"No," Isaac whispered, his voice breaking as he bent down to pick it up.

Standing over the vanity, leaning against the mirror he struggled to breath, desperate to find himself again. Wanting the pain to go away. Muttering to himself as he clutched the pills in his hands. Desperate for it all to end.

He clutched it in his palm, staring at it as if it held all the answers he was seeking. His breaths were shallow, his vision blurred by tears. The memories flooded back, Penelope lying in a hospital bed, the sound of the machines beeping, the feel of her hand in his.

Isaac, a voice echoed softly, faintly, from somewhere deep in his mind. It was a call he had heard countless times in his nightmares, whispering to him in the dark. Returning to the forest, the stench of death in his nose as he ran for his life in the darkness. Alone, he was always alone.

Isaac...

The room seemed to close in on him, the walls pressing in as the panic surged again. Isaac's fingers gripping the edge of the vanity for support. He could feel the baggie in his hand, it was now empty, the entirety of the contents gone. Isaac's body was hot, flooded with the surge of the high. It was too much, too sudden. His skin was on fire, ripping him apart from the inside.

"Please," he gasped, his voice choking with tears. "Penelope..."

"Isaac!"

The shout came from outside the door, a familiar voice, but it sounded so far away. Isaac was shaking, managing to stumble into the room, his head colliding with the plush carpet of the dressing room. Blinking bleary eyed as the door splintered open. Uncontrollable as his body spasmed, Isaac was choking on his own tongue as Thomas knelt beside him.

AFTER

SEPTEMBER 16, 1999 — 1:54 P.M.

D r. Fielder made a note in his book, the faint scratch of pen on paper the only sound breaking the silence. "Isaac," he began carefully, setting his pen aside, "your uncle has given us a very clear directive. He's concerned for your well being and believes you need more structured support."

Isaac's jaw tightened, his knuckles pressing against the fabric of the chair. "Structured support," he repeated, his voice dripping with disdain. "That's just a polite way of saying you're locking me up again."

The doctor didn't flinch at the accusation, his calm demeanor unshaken. "I know it feels that way. But this isn't about punishment, and it isn't about taking away your freedom. It's about giving you a chance to heal in a place where you'll be safe, with people who can help you."

Isaac's lips twisted into a bitter smile. "Safe. Sure. Because being locked behind padded walls, watched 24/7, and treated like some freak experiment is 'safe.'"

Dr. Fielder leaned forward slightly, his voice steady but firm. "I won't pretend this is an easy decision for anyone, least of all your uncle. But he wants what's best for you. Right now, you're barely holding yourself together, and that weight you carry—about Penelope, Henry, your mother—it's crushing you. If you stay in this limbo, Isaac, it'll only get worse."

The young man looked away, his jaw clenching and unclenching. "And what if I don't want to heal?" he muttered.

"Then that's something we'll have to work through," Dr. Fielder said without hesitation. "But no one is giving up on you. Not your uncle, not me, and not the staff at the institution. You may not believe it yet, but you're worth saving."

Isaac's laugh was short and hollow, devoid of humor. He sat back in the chair, his expression a mask of resignation. "So that's it? I don't get a choice?"

Dr. Fielder hesitated, then shook his head. "Not entirely, no. Your uncle has signed the paperwork, and I've provided my recommendation. But the institution isn't a prison, Isaac. It's a place where you can start to unpack everything you've been carrying—at your pace, on your terms."

The clock on the wall ticked steadily, its rhythm filling the space between them. Isaac didn't move, didn't speak. He simply stared at the floor, his thoughts unreadable.

"You'll have time to settle in," Dr. Fielder continued gently. "Your uncle will visit when you're ready, and I'll check in regularly. This isn't the end, Isaac. It's the beginning of something better."

Isaac's hands trembled as he pushed himself up from the chair. He stood for a moment, towering over the desk, his green eyes filled with a mix of anger and defeat. "Whatever you say, doc," he muttered before turning toward the door.

Dr. Fielder watched him go, his expression thoughtful. He reached for his notebook again, jotting down a few more notes before closing it with a sigh. As the door clicked shut behind Isaac, the doctor leaned back in his chair, steepling his fingers beneath his chin.

Outside the office, Isaac leaned heavily against the corridor wall, his shoulders hunched as he took a shaky breath. Ahead of him, two orderlies waited by the entrance, ready to escort him to the vehicle that would take him to the institution.

The young man straightened, fixing them with a glare as he walked toward them. His steps were slow but deliberate, his expression masking the turmoil churning inside him.

As they led him out of the building and into the waiting car, Isaac couldn't help but glance back at the hospital doors. Dr. Fielder's words echoed in his mind: "This isn't the end. It's the beginning of something better."